Inspired by the amazing true story of Winter

Dolphin Tale ™

Inspired by the amazing true story of Winter

Dolphin Tale:
The Junior Novel

Adapted by Gabrielle Reyes
Based upon the screenplay written by
Karen Janszen and Noam Dromi

SCHOLASTIC INC.

New York Toronto London Auckland
Sydney Mexico City New Delhi Hong Kong

ISBN 978-0-545-34842-3

12 11 10 9 8 7 6 5 4 3 2 1   11 12 13 14 15/0

Printed in the U.S.A.   40
First printing, August 2011

CHAPTER 1

S*PLASH!* Donovan Peck dove into the pool. His arms sliced through the water stroke after stroke. He paid no attention to Coach Vansky holding a stopwatch and barking instructions from the deck. He ignored the students and parents staring at him from alongside the pool. Within moments the high school senior had overtaken the swimmer next to him.

"This is the news with Sandra Sinclair. I'm poolside at the Long Center," said a pretty newswoman looking straight into the camera. "Last year, when nationally ranked swimming star Kyle Connellan graduated, he left behind five incredible State records. But now rising star Donovan Peck is now on the verge of smashing those records."

Sawyer looked up at his older cousin, Kyle, but Kyle's attention was focused on Donovan. "He's good, huh?" Kyle said as Donovan touched the finish on the opposite side of the pool. Coach Vansky clicked the stopwatch and looked at the time. He nodded. Impressed.

"Not as good as you," Sawyer responded. Kyle looked down and smiled at his eleven-year-old cousin and ruffled his hair. The two walked over to Coach Vansky.

"Kyle!" the coach called as if just noticing there were people outside of the pool. "How you doing?"

"Good." Kyle looked at the swim team gathering around Donovan. "Just dropped in to say my good-byes."

"So . . . you leave Monday, huh? Know where they're sending you yet?" Coach Vansky asked.

Sawyer looked down. He didn't want to think about his cousin leaving. He couldn't imagine not seeing him for a whole year. He couldn't even imagine getting through the summer. It was going to be bad enough going to summer school. But Kyle was practically his only friend. Without his cousin around to hang out with, it was going to be absolute torture.

"No sir," Kyle replied.

"Well, I hope they got a pool there. The Army's getting themselves one heck of a swimmer. . . ." The coach looked at his ex-student fondly. He went to shake Kyle's hand but gave him a huge hug instead. "I'm proud of you, son."

"Well, well . . ." Donovan interrupted, walking over while drying himself with a towel. "What brings you here, soldier-boy?" Sawyer noticed his cousin stand up a little straighter. Coach Vansky smiled at two of his best swimmers, then left to talk to his team.

Donovan gestured back to the pool with his head. "You catch my time?"

Sawyer knew his cousin had noted the time.

Kyle just shrugged.

"You know, while you're over there, you can kiss your records good-bye," continued Donovan.

Kyle pretended to look shocked. "Whoa, was that a challenge?"

Donovan grinned. "Any time. Any place."

"*That* would be a ratings grabber," noted a woman's voice.

The boys turned to see that Sandra the newscaster had been listening from nearby. She smiled as she stepped in between them.

"I'm sure everyone would love to see a race between Florida's two best young swimmers. I know the station would love it," she said.

Sawyer noticed his cousin adjust his shoulders making them seem even broader. "Sorry," said Kyle looking at Sandra. He was drawn in by her warm smile and the twinkle in her eye. "I'm shipping out in two days." For the first time, Sawyer got the feeling that Kyle wished he could stay home.

Sandra returned his gaze. "Oh. . . . That's too bad. How about a rain-check for when you get back?" she proposed.

"Sounds good," Kyle agreed.

"Care to comment for the news later?" Sandra pointed across the pool to the cameraman.

Kyle glanced at Donovan and smiled. "Nah, this is Donovan's story."

Sandra nodded. She started walking away but stopped to look back at Kyle. "I won't forget about that rain-check!" she called.

The next day, Kyle's mom, Alyce, and her sister, Lorraine, worked in the kitchen during Kyle's good-bye party.

"I should have known this day would come," said Alyce as she emptied a bag of chips into a bowl on the table. "His grandpa . . . then his dad . . . You're smart for not marrying the military," she said with a sigh.

Lorraine grabbed some bottles of soda to take out to the yard. "No," she muttered. "I just married a deserter."

Alyce hugged her sister. The sisters had always been there for each other's hard times and knew how to make each other feel better.

Lorraine looked through the window and watched Kyle and his friends throwing each other around in the pool. Then she noticed her son sitting off to the side playing a game on his cell phone. "Kyle's leaving isn't going to be easy for Sawyer. Kyle's like the big brother he never had. He's the only one who's ever been able to get Sawyer to come out of his shell."

As if knowing his mother was talking about him, Sawyer looked up from his game. He watched the members of the swim team joking around with his cousin in the pool. Then he stood up and left the yard.

Sawyer crossed the street and walked into the garage of his house. Bike parts, remote-controlled planes, and tools filled the workshop. Off to one side sat a laptop and large computer monitor. Sawyer sat down at his work bench and quietly started tinkering with a remote-control helicopter.

Sawyer was just about to test-fly the toy when his cousin walked in.

"Promise me you won't spend the whole summer in this place, ok?" Kyle asked.

Sawyer turned on the helicopter's motor. He shrugged as the rotors started up, adding a humming sound to the garage.

"I know you're not excited about having to go to summer school." Kyle gestured around him. "But at least it gets you out of this place. Promise me you'll go out and make some new friends, okay?"

Sawyer continued staring at the remote control in his hand.

But Kyle wasn't giving up. "Hey, look at me. I'm leaving. But this isn't like your dad. *I'm* coming back. And then we'll win some gold medals together at the Olympics, okay?"

Sawyer looked up. This was the part he didn't understand. "But why can't you stay and try out for the Olympics *now?*"

Kyle saw the sadness in his cousin's eyes. "It costs

money to train. But I do a little time in the Army and they'll pay for everything," he said gently.

Sawyer took this in. He wanted to understand, but he just couldn't.

"Listen, I got you something." Kyle handed his cousin a tissue-wrapped gift.

Sawyer got wide-eyed. He took the gift and opened it slowly. Inside the paper was a pocketknife. He ran his fingers over the case and pulled out the various tools. There were at least three different sized blades, a screwdriver, even a tiny pair of scissors. Sawyer turned the knife over and saw it was engraved: FAMILY IS FOREVER. He'd never gotten something so cool before. He was speechless.

"Now you can take your workshop with you wherever you go," Kyle explained. When he saw his little cousin smile for the first time in ages, he grinned and started for the door. "And you can start by using it to cut me a slice of my good-bye cake."

CHAPTER 2

y Monday morning, Kyle had left for the Army and Sawyer was pedaling his bike slowly down a dirt path by the shore. He was in no rush to get to his first day of summer school. After getting Ds and Fs in every subject except Shop, school was far from Sawyer's favorite place. He would much rather be building something in his workshop garage . . . or even out here staring into the water like that old fisherman was up ahead.

But what was *that fisherman staring at?* Sawyer wondered. He jolted when the fisherman turned to look right at him. "Hey! Hey, kid! You got a phone?" he shouted.

Sawyer slowed down his bike and looked at the old man with a confused expression.

"You got a phone?" the man repeated and gestured to something out on the water.

Sawyer stopped his bike completely, nodded, and came down the rocks. It was only then that he realized what had caught the fisherman's attention.

"911, what is your emergency?" came a voice from the cell phone.

The fisherman started describing his location, but Sawyer wasn't listening. Sawyer's eyes were taking in the gray-blue body of the animal lying on the sand, half in the water and half out.

A dolphin.

Sawyer kicked off his shoes and started to slowly approach the animal. The dolphin thrashed. Sawyer jumped back and held his breath. Then something else caught his eye. A crab trap's wire cage was pinned tightly around the dolphin's tail. A rope extending from the trap was wrapped around the dolphin's body and through its mouth. The animal thrashed again on the sand and landed in a new position on its side. Now Sawyer could see one of its blue eyes.

The boy could hardly breathe. While the fisherman paced the shore explaining the situation to the 911 operator, Sawyer kept his eyes locked on the dolphin's. Without even knowing what he was doing, he took out his pocketknife. "It's okay," he whispered. "I'm not going to hurt you."

The dolphin's eye followed Sawyer as he opened the knife and took a few steps closer. "Just hold on. I'm going to get this off of you." Sawyer walked down to the dolphin's tail and examined the wire trap. The trap door had to be opened in order to release the rope entangling the animal. Sawyer reached his fingers into the trap but he couldn't reach the release. He sat in the wet sand and used his feet to push the trap away from the dolphin's skin. Then he used the screwdriver to pry open the door.

Thwap!

The trap opened releasing the tension of the rope. With its head and mouth free, the dolphin could weakly turn its head to look at Sawyer. He had never seen such a beautiful animal this close. He laid a hand gently on the dolphin's body. It responded with a soft trilling sound.

A few minutes later, a large truck with the words *Clearwater Marine Hospital: Rescue-Rehab-Release* on its side pulled up to the shore. Dr. Clay Haskett stepped out of the cab with his eleven-year-old daughter, Hazel.

"Hazel, be careful!" he shouted after his daughter who was already running down to the beach. The rest of his team including two marine mammal specialists and a couple of volunteers quickly removed a video camera and a stretcher from the truck and began to follow her.

Down at the water, Hazel hurried toward Sawyer who was still kneeling by the dolphin's side. Hazel glanced from the dolphin's body, to the rope beside it, and then to the knife in Sawyer's hand. She opened her eyes wide. "Did you cut her free?" she asked.

Sawyer stood up self-consciously. He had just slipped the knife back into his pocket when Clay approached with two of the rescue workers.

Clay looked at the wounded animal and the ropes loosely wrapped around her. He studied the crab trap now stuck in the wet sand. "She was wrapped up in all this?" he asked the boy.

Sawyer remained silent but nodded. He stepped back as the rescue workers moved the dolphin out of the surf and Clay pulled the ropes off. One of the teenage volunteers recorded the workers as they examined the dolphin's shredded tail, poured ladles of water on its body, and covered it in wet towels.

A marine specialist named Phoebe addressed Sawyer. "How long was she out here?"

"I . . . I don't know," Sawyer stuttered. Hearing his voice, the dolphin made a trilling sound once again.

Hazel's eyes were glued to the dolphin. "She sounds like a bird, Dad," she noted.

She? thought Sawyer as they loaded the dolphin onto the stretcher. The crew worked together to lift it. When they passed Sawyer on the way to the truck, the dolphin trilled quietly. No one noticed but Hazel.

"Good work . . . ," she said looking at Sawyer. ". . . with the knife!" And she ran off to catch up with the others.

Sawyer looked up to the road where the animal was being loaded into the truck. He read the words painted on its side: Clearwater Marine Hospital.

CHAPTER 3

It was only when the Marine Hospital truck was out of sight that Sawyer remembered he was supposed to be at school. After the morning's excitement, Sawyer headed to class, but he could not concentrate. While his teacher, Mr. Doyle, droned on about prepositional phrases, all Sawyer could think about was the dolphin. *Was it—or rather,* she, *according to the girl—going to be all right?* Sawyer had to find out.

When the bell rang signaling the end of class, Sawyer was the first one out the door. He hopped on his bike and headed straight to the Clearwater Marine Hospital. Sawyer rode up to the blue two-story building with round concrete walls. He looked beyond the few cars in the parking lot and got a view of the big lagoon next to the hospital. As he got closer, he got off and walked his bike to the front door. According to the sign, the hospital was closed for the day. *But someone had to be taking care of the dolphin,* Sawyer thought. He decided to walk around to the back of the building to see if he could steal a look inside. Just as he had approached the back door, he heard footsteps. Somebody was coming! Sawyer ran and hid behind a big trash can. He peeked out to see the young girl from the beach exiting the door carrying a big box. Once she passed him and was out of sight, Sawyer dashed through the door.

Inside, Sawyer found himself in a long hallway. He wandered past various rooms with big tanks filled with brightly-colored fish. He stopped to watch a small shark lurking on the bottom of one tank. In another huge room, a giant manatee skeleton hung from the ceiling. Down the hall, an open tank held sea stars, hermit crabs, and sea cucumbers. It was a complete underwater world.

Sawyer was taking in all of the amazing creatures when a sound startled him.

ERP!

He whirled around to find a pelican barking at him from the middle of the floor.

"Shhh!" Sawyer whispered trying to shoo the bird away.

ARK! replied the pelican.

Afraid that someone would come to investigate, Sawyer rushed back toward the hallway—and ran SMACK into Hazel. Suddenly Sawyer was on the floor with the pelican and they both were surrounded by dead fish.

"Rufus, no!" scolded Hazel.

Hazel had been walking with a cooler full of fish to feed to the animals when Sawyer had run into her. Now fish were all over the floor, much to the delight of the pelican who was busy gulping them down.

Sawyer scrambled to help the young girl return the fish to the cooler.

"Bad, Rufus!" she said. She addressed Sawyer as she scooped up arms full of fish, "I named him Rufus 'cause he lives on the roof. Now he acts like he owns the place." Not only was Hazel not mad that Sawyer had snuck into the hospital, but she didn't even seem surprised. She paused and looked at the boy. "My name is Hazel, named after the eye-color."

Hazel waited for a few seconds expectantly. He finally responded, "Oh . . . I'm Sawyer." Then he straightened up and headed for the door.

"Wait. Where you going?" Hazel asked. "Don't you want to see the dolphin?"

Sawyer stopped.

"You're the boy from the beach, right?"

When Sawyer nodded, Hazel picked up the cooler and gestured to the doorway with her head. "Ok, but don't tell my dad. He doesn't want 'civilians' by the sick animals." The two headed for the stairs with the pelican skulking a few steps behind them.

"These fish were for the other two dolphins that are here, Krista and Panama. But now that they fell on the ground, we can't use them for their food. We're super careful with the fish the dolphins eat. Winter can't eat yet. She can barely move," Hazel explained.

Hazel was talking so fast, Sawyer had to struggle to keep up. "Winter?" he asked.

"That's what I named your dolphin. We had dolphins named Summer and Autumn here before. They got to go back to the ocean." Hazel stopped and tossed a look back at Sawyer. "So I figure season-names are good luck!"

When they got to the top of the stairs, they were on a concrete roof deck. Sawyer looked around to see a conference room, several offices, and a big pool. Hazel immediately brought him over to the pool. "That's Krista and that's Panama," she said pointing to two swimming dolphins. "Did you know dolphins need to be in a pool with at least one other dolphin? It's a law because they're so social. Like us," she noted and looked up at Sawyer. "Well, like *me* maybe. Everyone says I talk too much. . . ."

But Sawyer wasn't listening. He was fascinated by the dolphins that had swum right over to the edge of the pool.

"Did you know that dolphins use sonar?" Hazel chattered on. "They can practically see through things—but by using sound." She put down the cooler and lifted a heavy chair to set on top of it. Rufus the pelican tried to push the chair off using his beak. "They know this cooler is full of fish. *Shoo*, Rufus!" she commanded.

Hazel pulled Sawyer away and took him to a side wing of the hospital where there were two different sized pools. One was a four-foot-deep wading pool; next to it was a much bigger pool that was eight feet deep. The young girl pushed Sawyer behind a pillar and pointed. Inside the shallow pool, Phoebe, the marine mammal specialist, was wearing a wet suit and standing waist-deep in the water. In her arms she held the wounded dolphin, whose eyes were shut tight.

Sawyer watched mesmerized. He moved closer to get a better look and accidentally knocked over a broom.

Phoebe looked up hearing the clattering sound. "Hazel?"

Hazel and Sawyer stepped out sheepishly from behind the pillar. "Uh . . . Hi, Phoebe," Hazel said.

Phoebe glanced at Sawyer. "Honey, you know your dad doesn't like people back here."

Hazel started to explain. "I know, but . . . he's kinda the only reason Winter's even alive! He was the one who cut the ropes off of her."

"I . . . I just wanted to see how she was doing," Sawyer added.

Something made Phoebe look down to the water quickly. On hearing Sawyer's voice, Winter had shifted ever so slightly. She had opened her blue eyes and was looking in the boy's direction. "Well, she's in pretty bad shape," Phoebe said. "The circulation in her tail was cut off for quite a long time. There's lots of dead tissue. . . ."

Winter hadn't taken her eyes off Sawyer. Phoebe moved a bit so Winter could get a better view of the boy. "Is that better?" she asked the dolphin.

Winter surprised them by responding with a bird-like tweet. Just as Phoebe was about to remark on it, the three heard footsteps. Clay was coming down the hall.

"We gotta go!" Hazel said grabbing Sawyer by the arm. "Don't tell my dad, okay?" she pleaded to Phoebe and ran off.

After Hazel had snuck him out, Sawyer biked home. He immediately went to his garage workshop, turned on his computer, went to the search engine and typed "dolphin." He pored through page after page reading about everything from dolphins' use of sonar to their different types of vocalization. He watched videos of dolphins breaching, amazed at how far they could leap out of the water.

But the next day at school, all Sawyer watched was the clock waiting for class to end. As soon as class let out, Sawyer raced back to the Marine Hospital. Once again, he snuck through the back door making his way past the various tanks and up the stairs to the medical wing. He hid behind the same pillar as the day before and observed what was happening in the shallow pool.

This time, both Clay and Phoebe were in the water with Winter. Sawyer noticed that the dolphin's eyes were squeezed tightly shut. He was concentrating on Clay's examination of Winter's tail when Rufus squawked loudly.

ERP!

"Stop, no!" Sawyer whispered. "I don't have any fish—" He had crouched down to try to push the pelican away when he noticed a man's wet feet in front of him.

"Who are you?" said a man with a deep voice.

Sawyer looked up slowly.

"And how did you get in here?" the man interrogated.

Hazel rounded the corner with a cooler full of

fish and realized what was happening.

"He's the boy from the beach!" she said running over. "Remember, Dad?"

"I . . . I just . . ." Sawyer started to stammer.

Clay was just about to remind Hazel of the rules about visitors to this area of the hospital when Phoebe called out.

"Clay . . . she's awake."

Clay turned to look at Winter. Her eyes were open and she made a soft trilling sound.

"It's that bird sound," Hazel declared and pointed to Sawyer. "She makes that sound every time she sees him."

Winter wriggled weakly. Clay studied her and looked back to Sawyer. "Come here," he said. "It's okay," he added softening his voice when Sawyer hesitated.

Sawyer slowly walked over to the pool. Winter wiggled slightly.

"It's more than she's moved all day," Phoebe commented. Clay nodded to Phoebe who walked over to the pool's edge carrying Winter gently. Sawyer started to reach out his hand but stopped suddenly and looked at Clay.

"It's okay," he said. "Just be gentle."

Sawyer swallowed and reached out his hand. He touched Winter softly on the head. The dolphin sighed in Phoebe's arms.

Hazel looked up at her dad. "She really likes him . . . Is it okay if he comes back, Dad?"

Clay's eyes had been locked on the dolphin but now he turned to look at his daughter. "Maybe . . . yeah, sure."

Everyone was quiet for a moment when—

BRRRAAAP!

Winter made a loud raspberry sound! Clay, Phoebe, Hazel, and Sawyer burst out laughing.

"I guess Winter likes the sound of that," said Hazel with a big smile.

CHAPTER 4

*T*he next morning, Sawyer hopped on his bike as usual. But this time instead of riding to school, he rode right past it. At the Marine Hospital, he went through the back door without hesitation. He couldn't wait to see Winter. When he got inside, he noticed that the halls were quieter than usual. No one was in the gift shop. He peeked into the kitchen but it was empty. Sawyer climbed the stairs to the deck and saw Krista and Panama swimming around in their pool unattended. *Where was everyone?* Sawyer wondered. When he heard a muffled sound he looked towards the corner. Hazel was sitting on the floor with tears streaming down her face.

Sawyer rushed over. "Hazel . . . ? What is it?"

Hazel was too choked up to answer. Sawyer glanced around and noticed Clay and Phoebe standing in the shallow pool. He looked past them into the water and realized Winter's tail was gone. Just a stump was left where her tail should have been. Sawyer gasped. "What happened?!?" he cried.

Clay sighed. "It had to come off. The infection had spread too far and she wouldn't have survived. . . ."

Sawyer was in disbelief. "But how can she swim without a tail?"

"If she can't swim," Hazel sniffed. "She'll die. . . ."

Clay looked at the two forlorn kids. "I'm sorry, honey," he said addressing his daughter. He looked back to Sawyer. "We had no choice . . . At least this way, she has more of a chance."

* * *

Sawyer pushed his bike along as he walked with Hazel. For once, Hazel didn't feel much like talking. The two went past the cars in the parking lot and past the boats docked along the lagoon finally stopping in front of a houseboat with a shingled roof.

"Want a lemonade icicle before you go home?" Hazel asked. "I make them myself," she added half-heartedly.

"No thanks," Sawyer muttered. He didn't feel much like eating.

"Nothing goes down with bad news like one of my granddaughter's lemonade icicles." Hazel's grandfather Reed had come out to stand on the deck of their houseboat. "Come on in," he said to the kids. "I'm buying."

Hazel showed Sawyer around the inside cabin. It was filled with various shell collections and artifacts from all over the world. Sawyer eyed a cabinet full of carved figures. "Did your dad carve all those?" he asked. "Are they, like, whale bone or something?"

"Close," Hazel replied. "Beef bone—from the grocery store."

Reed came out of the kitchen holding two icicles and Hazel led them out to the back deck of the boat. They licked the frozen treats from deck chairs and gazed out at the boats along the marina.

"Have you always lived near the water?" Sawyer asked.

Hazel nodded. "My grandpa says we have salt water in our veins. When my dad was little, the two of them sailed all over the world." Hazel turned to look at her friend. "What does your dad do?"

Sawyer shrugged. "I don't know . . . He left five years ago and we're not really sure where he is now. Never calls. Never writes."

"Oh." Hazel was speechless.

"How about your mom?" he asked trying to change the subject.

"Oh," said Hazel looking back at the water. "She died when I was seven." She turned back to look at Sawyer. "Never calls. Never writes." The two smiled at each other and shrugged. "C'mon," she said getting to her feet and pointing up. "I'll show you the crow's nest." She walked over to a ladder and started to climb. "This is where I do all my homework—I'm homeschooled. Do you like school?"

Sawyer followed Hazel to the crow's nest located at the top of the boat's mast. It was just like a tree fort but on the water. He shrugged again. "I fail almost every class."

The two took in the full view of all of the boats on the marina. "You probably just haven't found a subject that interests you yet," Hazel said knowingly.

Sawyer had never thought about school that way before. In the distance they could hear Krista and Panama's vocalizing. They sounded playful with each other. "Is Winter going to die?" Sawyer asked.

Hazel bit her lip. "I hope not . . ." she said softly. "When we rescue an animal, we always try to save it. We always try. . . ."

* * *

"We *have* to get her to eat." Clay was upset when Sawyer next visited. The veterinarian stood in the pool with Hazel nearby and Phoebe supporting Winter. He held a big contraption attached to a clear hose. Sawyer watched intently as Clay inserted the tube into the dolphin's mouth. As orange liquid flowed through the tube, Hazel explained, "We're trying to get her to eat. The food is orange so we can tell if she spits it out."

In a moment the water was cloudy and orange. Winter refused to eat. "Let's give it a rest," Clay said with a sigh. He walked over to the edge of the pool and noticed Sawyer nearby. He got an idea. "Can you swim?" he asked gruffly.

A few minutes later, Sawyer was stepping into the pool. He wore a pair of swimming trunks that were too big for him and a T-shirt from one of the volunteers. He waded over to Clay, Hazel, and Winter self-consciously.

"Just put your hands under her, like Hazel," Clay instructed.

Sawyer watched where Hazel was putting her hands and did the same. As he put his hands on Winter, the dolphin fluttered her eyes open. She craned her neck a bit to see him, then shut her eyes again and sighed.

Clay was amazed. "Let her rest on you. Make sure her blow hole is above the water."

Sawyer adjusted his arms. Winter nestled against him laying her head on his chest.

"Now—just walk her around slowly," said Clay stepping back.

Hazel and Sawyer held their breaths while carefully moving Winter through the water. She made a faint trilling sound.

Clay checked his watch, sighed, and got out of the pool. Winter seemed to be making some progress. He wished he could stay where he was. "Got the board meeting . . . Keep an eye on them," he said to Phoebe. Clay glanced back at the pool, "I'll see you kids later."

But the only one who had Sawyer and Hazel's attention was Winter.

* * *

Around the table, the Clearwater Marine Hospital's board of directors went over the pile of documents in front of them. From the window, Rufus could be seen sitting on a railing outside.

"We're not panicking—yet." Gloria Forrest was seventy-three and the president of the board. She looked up from the paperwork. "We've lost our two biggest government grants in the past six months and it's left us swimming in debt," she announced to the room. "Pardon the pun."

"There is some good news," John Fitch, another board member noted. "We have a strong offer on the table."

Clay pushed back his chair and stood up. "Can I go back to work?"

"We have to consider it, Clay," John replied. He held a brochure in his hands. On the cover were photographs of resort hotels and the CEO of Hordern Development and Investments, Philip J. Hordern. "He's not a bad guy. He's interested in buying the property, but he's also willing to pay for the costs of relocating all the animals."

Clay scoffed. "Because that's just what Florida needs. Another hotel."

John continued. "We could wipe out all of our debts." He looked up at Clay. "*And* get the animals placed. . . ." The two men held each other's gazes.

"There's still time," Christina Hong, the board member sitting between them broke in. "Maybe a corporate sponsor will step up."

Gloria looked out the window deep in thought and sighed. "Or maybe Rufus will win the lottery."

After Clay stormed out of the board meeting, he returned to the pool. Phoebe, Sawyer, and Hazel had blended together goat's milk, fish, and antibiotics into a kind of shake for Clay to feed to Winter. He poured the fish stew into a big plastic bottle and slid a rubber nipple on top. "Bring her closer," he said to Hazel and Sawyer when they were all in the water.

Hazel and Sawyer worked together to glide Winter over to Clay. "Come on, Winter. Open up," he said.

But Winter didn't move. Clay looked at her with a frown. "I guess we'll have to try the tube again."

"Why don't you let Sawyer try?" Reed had come to see how Winter was doing and stood by the edge of the pool. Clay considered his father's idea. Reed caught his eye and gave him a look. *Why not?*

Clay shrugged and passed the bottle to Sawyer. Winter's eyes fluttered opened when she heard Sawyer ask, "What do I do?"

"Hold the bottle up to her eye and show it to her," Clay instructed.

Winter looked at the bottle and sighed. But she still wouldn't take it.

"Talk to her," suggested Clay.

Sawyer didn't know what to do. He looked helplessly from Clay to Reed. Reed gave a supporting nod. "Go ahead."

"Um . . . okay." The boy turned his attention to the animal in his arms. "Come on, Winter," he whispered. "I know you feel lousy . . . but you have to eat. If you don't eat, you'll never get better."

Winter grunted. Phoebe and some of the other hospital workers came out onto the deck to see what was going on.

"It's good," Sawyer continued. "Hazel made it herself." He pretended to suck on the bottle. "See? Mmmm. Delicious."

Winter responded with a loud raspberry sound, *BRRRAAAP!*

Everyone laughed except Clay. He was watching Winter intently.

"My dad's jealous," Hazel said with a smile. "Usually *he's* the favorite."

Sawyer glanced around and noticed more and more people had come to watch. "See, Winter. Everyone's here rooting for you." But Winter still wouldn't take the bottle. Sawyer thought of their first meeting on the beach. He remembered Winter's first sound when he cut off the rope and he began to whistle softly.

Sawyer could see Winter looking at him with one

of her blue eyes. A moment later, she whistled back. Slowly holding the bottle out, Sawyer cooed. "Come on . . . you can do it."

Winter looked at the bottle. She bumped the nipple with her rostrum, the beak-like part of her face. She looked back at Sawyer and opened her mouth to take in the nipple. She paused, then squeaked, and took a long pull.

Sawyer had been holding his breath. "Atta girl," he said and exhaled.

No one moved as they all watched Winter feed. When the bottle was empty, the dolphin yanked it from Sawyer's grip. She flipped it high into the air and it landed on the deck by Phoebe.

"She wants more!" Hazel shouted.

"Okay," Clay said gruffly. "Maybe I am a *little* jealous."

Sawyer looked up at Clay. He had never felt so happy. And for the first time since Sawyer met him, he even saw Clay smile.

CHAPTER 5

*H*i, Mom! Hi, Uncle Max! Hi, Aunt Alyce!" Sawyer barreled through the door, dropped his back pack, and ran into the kitchen where his family was sitting. After successfully feeding Winter, Sawyer was filled with energy.

"There you are," his mother Lorraine said looking at him intently. "How was school?"

Uh-oh. Sawyer thought. Sawyer's days had been full of excitement. He felt like he was learning more than he ever had in his whole life. But it hadn't been at school. "Um . . . fine." he answered.

"Oh?" Lorraine raised her eye brows. "That's interesting. Because your teacher Mr. Doyle called and said you haven't been there for a week."

Sawyer froze. Before he could think of what to say, his mother burst out.

"What is that *stench*?"

The words came rushing out of Sawyer's mouth. He explained that he was covered in the fish shake that he and Hazel had fed to Winter. But then he realized he had to go back and tell his mom who Hazel was. And how he met her after he had rescued Winter. And how he was the only one who could get Winter to eat. His mother could barely keep up with him. She was furious. But all she cared about at the moment was getting him into the shower.

Half an hour later, Sawyer came back into the kitchen fresh from the shower. Lorraine took one whiff. "Get back in there," she said and pointed back to the bathroom door. Max and Alyce sat at the table quietly, trying to be invisible.

"Fine, but I can't go back to school tomorrow," Sawyer gushed. "I have to go back to—"

"Enough. We are not discussing it, Sawyer."

"But mom, Winter needs me. If I stop now—"

"You are going back to school. Period!"

Lorraine glared at her son. Sawyer felt a lump building in his throat. Before he burst into tears in front of everyone, he turned and ran down the hall to his room where he slammed the door.

Lorraine sighed and caught the look being exchanged between Alyce and Max. "What?" she asked them.

Max shrugged. "I didn't say anything. I'm just the uncle."

"What is it, Max?" she insisted.

"It's just . . . it's hard to remember the last time the boy was this excited about something."

"I must be out of my mind." Lorraine said to herself as she drove with Sawyer the next day. "You cannot just disappear and spend an entire week at a place full of strangers." She looked at Sawyer shifting in his seat. His seatbelt was tucked under his arm. "And put your seatbelt on right. How many times do I have to tell you?"

Sawyer grabbed the seatbelt and made a face. "It rubs," he complained.

"I don't care if it rubs," Lorraine said exasperated. "That's better then you ending up . . ." Lorraine struggled to find the right words but gave up. "And anyway, we don't know anything about these people, Sawyer. You could have drowned, or been stabbed, or heaven only knows what." They pulled into the hospital's driveway. Lorraine studied the dilapidated building. "Is *this* it?"

Sawyer nodded and burst out, "It used to be a sewage treatment plant before they converted it. Cool, huh?"

Lorraine made a face and had just stopped the car when Sawyer hopped out. "Sawyer, wait—"

But it was too late. Sawyer had already rushed off to the main door. Lorraine sighed, grabbed her purse, and followed her son. She took in her surroundings as she walked through the parking lot. Next to the hospital building were empty plastic pools, discarded equipment, and dirty tarps.

ERP!

Lorraine clutched her bag to her and jumped back a step. Rufus stretched his big wings and flapped at her. "Oh, for heavens sake," she said as she rolled her eyes. She ran to the front door with the pelican on her heels.

Sawyer's mom entered the building through the main entrance and met up with Sawyer who was already inside. He led her through the rooms with the tanks full of tropical fish, turtles, and sharks.

"Morning, Sawyer," said one of the tour guides.

"Hi, Virginia," he replied. He ran across the hall to the turtles. "That's Peanut-Butter and that's Jelly," he stated. "They're green sea turtles. You can touch them if you want."

"Uh, that's ok. I'm good," said his mother backing away.

The mother and son went through each room. Sawyer shared everything he had learned about all the animals. Together they stood watching the otters at the otter pool. "These were all either sick or injured. We're teaching them to catch their own fish, so we can release them back in the wild. They're cute, but if you put your finger in there, they could bite it right off."

A moment passed then Sawyer was off again. "Let's go meet Krista and Panama!" Sawyer led his mom to the viewing windows of the dolphin pool. "From these windows, you can see under the water where the dolphins swim," Sawyer noted.

Lorraine moved her face close to the windows and looked through the clear blue water. "I don't see anything."

Suddenly, Krista glided right past. Lorraine gasped and pulled back from the window. Panama joined Krista and the two stared through the glass.

"That's Panama," Sawyer said proudly. "She's old . . . She can't catch fish anymore because she's deaf and dolphins echo-locate, you know?" Lorraine's response was a puzzled expression, but Sawyer was already moving on. "Krista was run over by a boat but as soon as she heals, we can send her home. Cool, right?"

Lorraine was amazed at how the words spilled out of Sawyer. It was the first time in ages that she had seen her son so eager. And everyone knew him—the tour guides, the gift shop cashiers, the animal specialists who fed and took care of the animals all greeted Sawyer happily. Her son had never looked more at home.

At the medical pool, Phoebe and another marine specialist were in the water holding Winter afloat as Clay fed her a bottle.

"And that's Winter," Sawyer announced. Lorraine noticed the gentle tone of concern in his voice.

Reed came over and shook Lorraine's hand. "Welcome. We've heard so much about you," he said warmly.

Lorraine glanced over at her son. It was hard to stay mad when she saw how happy he was in this place. She turned back to Reed and smiled. "I . . . wish I could say the same."

Reed returned the smile and introduced Lorraine to the rest of the crew. "That's my son Clay, my granddaughter Hazel, and Phoebe and Kat our dolphin specialists."

"We'd shake hands," Clay said from the water, but then shrugged and looked down at his hands which were full cradling Winter.

Lorraine looked at the wounded animal. The dolphin looked so vulnerable in the water. "Can she swim without a tail?" she asked.

"That's the big question," Phoebe replied.

"How old is she?" asked Lorraine with concern.

"Just a kid," Sawyer answered. "Dolphins stay with their moms for years though."

"Now Sawyer's her mother," Reed noted.

Lorraine laughed until she realized that he was serious.

Sawyer looked at his mother hopefully.

"Oh, Sawyer . . ." she said. "I don't know what to say. . . ."

"Please, Mom," Sawyer begged. "I'll take extra classes next year. Or I'll write an essay or a report. I'll do anything they want—"

But Lorraine wasn't sure. *Maybe her son was right and the dolphin really did need him. Maybe Winter knew how special her son was. But what if the staff didn't want Sawyer around? Was it okay that he spent his summer here with them?* She looked at Clay. He seemed to have read her thoughts. He nodded.

Lorraine inhaled. "Okay—I get it," she said finally. "I'll talk to Mr. Doyle and—"

But before she could finish Sawyer had thrown his arms around her.

"I'm sorry. But no."

After leaving her son at the Marine Hospital, Lorraine drove over to his school to talk to Mr. Doyle. She stood in his classroom in front of the board listing columns of adjectives and adverbs and had explained to her son's teacher how Sawyer had rescued a dolphin and how she had never seen him so interested in learning before. But the teacher stood firm.

"If we allow this, how is it fair to the other kids whose summer I'm ruining?" he countered.

"But that's the point," Lorraine argued. "My son is having the best summer he's ever had—and he's *learning*. He's willing to do whatever it takes. Let him write an essay. Give him a report. This experience is more valuable than anything you could possibly teach him."

Mr. Doyle bristled. "I'm a very good teacher. I'm sure your son would learn plenty if he actually attended class."

Lorraine realized that she might have insulted Mr. Doyle. "I didn't mean that. . . . Look, I wasn't happy about it either. But I just saw something in my son that a mother—a teacher—dreams of seeing. He's excited. He's engaged. And not with a video game. He cares about something alive—and it needs him."

Mr. Doyle brought his hand to his chin and paused for a moment. Finally he looked Sawyer's mother in the eye. "If he wants credit for the class . . . he has to *be* in the class. I'm sorry."

"You should be," she said, holding his gaze. And she turned and walked out the door.

*　*　*

When Sawyer came home that evening, Lorraine was doing the dishes in the kitchen. He dropped his backpack and walked over to the kitchen table. There was a plate of food set for him beside a big gift box. He looked up at his mother who just shrugged. Sawyer slowly opened the box. Inside was a wet suit in his size. Sawyer looked up at his mom with wide-eyes. On top of the wet suit was a note: "Your new school uniform. Love, Mom." For the second time that day, Lorraine was crushed by a huge hug from her son.

CHAPTER 6

Your mom seems really nice," Hazel chattered while holding Winter. Sawyer was wearing his new wet suit and trying to feed Winter a bottle. The dolphin yanked the bottle away and tossed it aside. "C'mon, Winter. Don't be a brat," Hazel teased.

Sawyer sighed. He grabbed the bottle and tried again. Winter ignored it, took a mouthful of water and squirted it at him. "Cut it out, Winter!" he scolded wiping his face.

Hazel laughed. "Boy, she's really in a mood today."

Winter squirmed in Hazel's arms and thrashed from side to side. "Winter, stop it," she said trying to hang on to the dolphin. But Winter didn't listen. She thrashed one more time and squirmed right out of Hazel's grasp. "Hey—" she said trying to chase after the animal.

"Wait. Look." Sawyer pointed at the dolphin. Winter was wiggling her stump from side to side and paddling with her pectoral fins. Sawyer was amazed. "She's . . . she's swimming."

Hazel stood perfectly still and watched breathlessly. "Dad! DAD!" she shouted. Clay and Phoebe ran out of their offices. Hazel pointed at Winter who was still thrashing in the water and wiggling her stump from side to side. She was flapping her fins frantically. But she was keeping herself afloat.

Clay gaped at the animal. "She's wiggling like a snake," he said in shock.

"Or a shark," Phoebe observed.

Everyone watched with delight as Winter made

her way back into Hazel's arms. The dolphin made her contented bird sound.

"Good job, Winter," Hazel said petting the dolphin. "Good job!"

Winter's improvements energized Sawyer and Hazel. They wanted to learn everything that was involved in running the Marine Hospital. Every day they worked together to make Winter her fish shakes and feed them to her. Reed showed Sawyer how to fix the filter pumps for the wading pool. When one of the turtles swallowed a fish hook, Clay and Phoebe taught the kids how to read an X-Ray. When Sawyer wasn't at the Marine Hospital, he was at home researching marine animals or working in the garage. He gathered pool toys, a foam mattress, and inflatable balls—anything he could think of that might inspire Winter to move around and regain her strength. Sometimes, the kids would lie on floats in the pool with Winter floating on a mattress beside them. Sawyer had never been happier.

"Mom, I'm home!" he shouted bouncing into the kitchen one evening. He stopped when he realized his mother was sitting at the kitchen table with his Aunt Alyce. Both of the women were crying. He looked to his mother. "What . . . what is it? Is it Kyle?"

His mother lifted a tissue to dry her eyes. "He's hurt, honey. There was an explosion." Her eyes filled up again. "They say it's bad."

"Is he going to be okay?" Sawyer asked his aunt.

"They think so . . ." Alyce said through her tears. "He's coming home."

Later that evening, Clay stood on the dock looking at his daughter and her friend. She and Sawyer sat together on the back deck of his houseboat silently staring at the other boats in the marina. He took a deep breath and climbed onto the boat. "I . . . heard about your cousin," he said putting his hand on Sawyer's shoulder. "He's alive. . . . That's what matters. . . ."

Sawyer nodded. The three were quiet. "He

doesn't want to come home and see us," Sawyer said not taking his eyes off the water. "He just wants to go straight to the VA hospital."

Clay and Hazel looked at each other. They could both see how hurt Sawyer was. They wanted to help but didn't know how.

"Hm . . ." Clay thought. "How would you two like to be on the night shift tonight? Help keep an eye on Winter for me?"

Sawyer snapped to attention. "Really?!"

Clay took in the two hopeful faces in front of him. "Really."

In a couple of hours, Sawyer and Hazel were settled into their sleeping bags on the roof deck of the hospital. Clay did one last check-in with Phoebe who was sitting on the pool's edge petting Winter. Then he came over to sit with the kids.

"Doctor—" Sawyer started.

"I think it's okay to call me Clay," the doctor said sitting in a chair beside them.

Sawyer nodded. "Clay . . ." He began again tentatively. "Do you think Winter remembers things? Like the ocean? Or her family?"

Clay took something small out of his pocket and began carving it with a knife. After a moment he said, "Hard to say. . . . They're pretty smart. A lot of people think they're smarter than we are."

"Some people think dolphins actually *are* people," Hazel chimed in.

Sawyer was puzzled.

"In California, the Chumash Indians have a legend," Clay explained. "Long ago, their goddess, Hutash, wanted them to move off the islands where they lived, onto the mainland. So she made a bridge for them out of a rainbow. But as they were crossing over, some of the kids started fooling around—just being kids."

Hazel and Sawyer looked at each other and smiled.

"Some of the kids fell off the rainbow and went tumbling towards the sea," Clay continued. "The parents were terrified that Hutash would be angry with them and let the children drown. But Hutash loved how they played. So she took pity on them. The moment they hit the water, she turned them into dolphins so they could play forever."

Hazel's dad tossed the small carving to Sawyer. The boy caught it and looked down in his hand. In his palm was a little bone carving of a dolphin—with no tail.

At midnight, Hazel and Phoebe were sound asleep in their sleeping bags. But Sawyer sat on the edge of the deep pool playing with the dolphin carving. Winter came over and nudged his feet with her rostrum.

"Do you miss your family?" the boy asked the animal. "You know. . . my cousin Kyle is hurt. We don't know how bad yet." He kicked his feet in the water. "He's a swimmer. Fast, too."

Winter squeaked.

"Well, fast for a human. But he's strong like you. So he's gonna be fine. You both are." Sawyer took a bottle from a cooler nearby. "Want a snack?"

Winter responded with a loud raspberry sound.
BRAAAPPP!

"Guess not . . ." Sawyer went to put the bottle back in the cooler when—

SPLOOSH!

"Winter!" Sawyer's back was totally drenched. Winter had squirted him with a mouthful of water. The dolphin made a bubbly sound and slowly dipped her head below the water's surface. Sawyer grabbed a towel and rubbed it on his hair.

SPLAT!

Winter had soaked him *again*.

"Aw, cut it out!" Sawyer told his underwater friend.

BRRRRR!

Winter made a motorboat sound and dove under the water once more. The boy couldn't help but laugh. "Okay, so you want to play?" He grabbed a yellow floating ring toy and held it out to her. Winter swam over, sniffed, and swam away. "Come on. . . . Do you want it or not?" Sawyer asked getting frustrated again. He held it out farther. The dolphin squealed. She wiggled over and lunged for the ring. She grabbed it with her mouth and swam back—yanking Sawyer right into the water.

"Aaah!"

Sawyer tried to get his footing in the pool, but Winter bumped him playfully and knocked him over.

"Winter, stop!" he said with a scowl.

But Winter just splashed him again. Sawyer had had enough. He scooped handfuls of water and splashed Winter right back. It was just what Winter wanted. Play time! She flapped her fins wildly, splashing Sawyer all over. As fast as he splashed back, it was no match for Winter.

"Okay, okay! I surrender!" Sawyer sputtered. He struggled to his feet and wiped his wet face. Winter nudged his hand with her rostrum. Sawyer looked down at the animal and pet her head gently. He whistled softly to her and she echoed the sound back to him. Then she squealed, nudged him again, and darted away. She wanted him to chase her! Sawyer ducked under the water and swam after Winter. Under the water she blew a ring of bubbles and she and Sawyer swam right through it. Winter twirled onto her back and gestured to Sawyer with her fin. When she flipped back over, Sawyer took her top dorsal fin and Winter pulled him in a big circle around the pool. *Whoosh!*

Clay hadn't known how to cheer up Sawyer.

But he knew Winter would.

CHAPTER 7

A couple of days later, Sawyer hopped out of the truck and glanced at the words painted on the side: Rescue-Rehab-Release. He shut the door and gathered with the rest of the team at the back of the truck. Everyone was energetic. It was time to release Krista back to the ocean.

Clay and the others lifted the stretcher and carried Krista down to the water.

"Watch your footing, keep her level—" Phoebe directed.

"Careful of the flukes," Clay added.

Krista wiggled with excitement.

"Easy now, Krista. Easy. Time to go home," Phoebe said soothingly.

The team waded out waist-deep into the water with the stretcher.

"That's it. Far enough," Phoebe declared.

Krista gave a snap of her tail, making Hazel jump. "Whoa, look out!" she warned.

"Okay," Phoebe instructed. "Here we go. Everybody: One, two, three—lift!"

Clay and the others raised the stretcher while Phoebe carefully rolled Krista towards her. She cradled the dolphin until she was in the water.

SPLASH!

Clay moved next to Phoebe. "That's it, Krista," Phoebe said. "Go on home."

The dolphin rolled in the water. She hesitated, getting used to the feeling of the ocean around her.

"Dad—" Hazel pointed at something off in the distance. "Look!"

A dolphin
is hurt!

Rescue
workers help
the dolphin.

Sawyer visits Winter to see how she is doing.

Winter is happy to see her friend Sawyer.

Winter and Sawyer swim together.

Playtime for Winter, Sawyer, and Hazel.

Rufus annoys Sawyer . . . again!

Sawyer and Hazel make fish milkshakes for Winter. Yuck!

Sawyer is the only person that can get Winter to eat.

Dr. Haskett tells Sawyer and Hazel that Winter may be in danger.

Sawyer is worried about Winter—she may never swim again.

Sawyer can always turn to his cousin Kyle for advice.

Dr. McCarthy shows off Winter's new tail.

Dr. Haskett puts on Winter's new tail.

Winter tries out her new tail.

Sawyer has fun with all his friends at the Save Winter event.

Everyone turned their attention away from Krista and looked out to the horizon. Two dolphins were breaching. The water spread apart in huge circles as the dolphins fell back into the water. Moments later they were swimming towards Krista.

Sawyer, Hazel, and the others watched wide-eyed. Krista gave a small push with her tail propelling herself forward just a bit. She looked ahead and let out a high-pitched squeal. A chorus of whistles echoed in response. The two dolphins in the distance had joined their pod. Krista's squeals got louder and louder. She gave a happy slap of her flukes and rolled onto her back. She looked at Clay, Phoebe, and the kids.

Hazel tugged on her father's arm. "Is that her family?"

Clay smiled and put a hand on his daughter's back. "You never know."

"I think it is. I think that's her family and they're coming for her."

Krista flapped her pectoral fins still floating in front of the group.

"I think . . ." Sawyer looked into Krista's eyes. ". . . she's saying good-bye," said Sawyer.

As if confirming, Krista let out a loud squeal. Then she turned back over and dove down into the water. She gave a big push with her tail then wiggled her body with full-force propelling herself forward and out of sight. Before long, the group saw Krista surface. One by one, her pod surfaced around her, their faces bobbing in the water. Excited squealing filled the air.

Hazel lifted her arm and started to wave. Clay wrapped his arm around her shoulder as the team watched Krista and her pod jump, arc over the water, and dive back in over and over again until they were out of sight. Krista was home.

"Cross your fingers. You never know . . ." Clay worked the hoist as Phoebe gave hand signals. Now that Krista was back in the wild, the team was putting Winter in the deeper pool with Panama. "Let's just hope they get along."

As Clay worked the machine to lower the stretcher, Hazel and Sawyer helped the others steady it from inside the pool. Reed watched from the deck while one of the volunteers recorded the transfer.

Clay smiled as Phoebe directed the team, "Just a little lower . . . a little bit more."

"Dr. Clay," said Sawyer looking at Winter's stump. "What's that lump on her back?"

In the middle of Winter's back near the end of her stump was a large bulge.

"Yeah, I saw that. I'm not sure," Clay replied. "We'll have to take a look."

On Phoebe's instructions, the team gently eased Winter off of the stretcher. She lightly splashed into the new pool. Phoebe and the others swam to the edge leaving Winter hovering in the middle of the water. In a moment, Panama joined Winter at the surface. The animals eyed each other.

Sawyer whispered. "Why aren't they moving?"

"What if Panama doesn't like her?" Hazel added.

"Shhh," said Clay.

Panama made a clicking sound. She was echo-locating on Winter's stump. Agitated, she swam off in a big circle. Winter wiggled her tail side-to-side moving herself to the edge of the pool.

Sawyer furrowed his brow. "Why is Panama swimming laps?"

"She does that when she's upset," answered Kat, one of the dolphin specialists.

Over and over again, Panama swam in big circles while Winter waited off to the side. Suddenly Panama dove under the water, then she pushed herself towards the surface. With a burst of energy, she breached high above the water's surface and landed with a big splash. Her agitation turned to anger. She started smacking her tail hard.

"Let's get Winter out!" Phoebe ordered.

Clay held her back. "Not yet. Just wait."

But Panama kept smacking her tail. When she finally stopped, she was breathing hard.

Winter looked to the other animal and swam right over to her. With no hesitation, Winter nuzzled the dolphin and made a soft whistling sound. Panama floated motionless.

Phoebe looked at Clay. "She's not rejecting," she said sounding relieved.

Winter wiggled away from Panama moving her stump from side to side. Panama watched her for a few seconds, then swam forward to join her. The animals swam next to each other squeaking back and forth. And the team exhaled.

"See?" Clay said with a grin. "Piece of cake."

Seeing Krista return to her family reminded Sawyer how much he missed his cousin. He couldn't wait to tell Kyle all about Winter and the other animals at the Marine Hospital. Kyle would be so proud of him for making such great new friends, like Hazel, Phoebe, and Clay. He climbed up to the crow's nest of Hazel's houseboat and tried to call Kyle at the VA hospital. But his cousin still wouldn't take any calls. Sawyer hung up the phone and put it in his lap. Just then he saw one of his remote-controlled helicopters rising up.

Hazel was waving his toy in the air as she climbed into the crow's nest.

"You promised you'd teach me to fly it, remember?" Hazel looked down at the cell phone in her friend's lap. She could tell by Sawyer's expression that he hadn't been able to get through to Kyle. "Maybe it'll cheer you up. Or we could just sit here. But that doesn't seem nearly as fun," she teased.

Her tactic worked. Sawyer grabbed the helicopter with both hands. "Okay, let's go," he said.

In the parking lot, Sawyer directed Hazel to put the helicopter on the ground and step back. "Okay, I'll get it in the air, then you can fly it."

Hazel nodded eagerly.

"If you're careful," he added.

Sawyer nudged the controller and the helicopter motor revved. It ascended into the air and hovered around them.

"Lift off!" Hazel exclaimed. "That is so cool!"

Sawyer kept his eyes on the helicopter. With small pushes to the controller, it smoothly veered left and right. The kids watched it hover just inches above the parked cars and trace their surfaces. "Okay, just use little movements," Sawyer explained. "This is up, down, and this is sideways."

Hazel held out her hands. "Let me try!"

Sawyer handed her the remote. She grabbed the joystick making the helicopter wobble. When she shot the joystick forward, the helicopter lurched.

"Sweet, I'm doing it!"

"Watch it, easy. . . ." Sawyer cautioned.

But Hazel was just getting started. She yanked the joystick the other way making the helicopter fly straight up into the air.

"Oops," she said.

Sawyer held out his hand. "Hazel, not like that. Here, give it to me—" He grabbed the controller. *Zoom!* The toy zipped up even higher into the air and right over the top of the aquarium building.

Hazel watched the helicopter disappear over the roof. She looked at her friend, bracing herself. "Um . . . sorry?"

Sawyer thumbed the controller frantically. "Where is it? Do you see it?"

Hazel flinched. "Did you put, like, a 'Come home' button on it?"

Sawyer shot her a look. *Girls,* he thought. He turned his attention back to the controller working the joystick.

"I would've put a 'Come home' button on it," Hazel muttered.

Meanwhile, the helicopter was buzzing over the dolphins on the deck of the hospital. It bounced off a wall and veered toward the otter house. The otters stood on their hind legs fascinated by what looked like an oversized dragonfly. It was coming right at them! They dove out of the way, tumbling over each other into one big heap.

Next the flying toy rounded the corner and dive-bombed the turtles, who ducked their heads back into their shells. Intrigued by the motor's noise, Winter bobbed her head up from the water. She squealed watching the helicopter zip past.

ERP! For once, Rufus wasn't chasing anything. But the copter was chasing him! He flapped his wings wildly as the helicopter headed straight for him. *WHOOSH!* The propellers just missed him but they sent a flurry of feathers flying into the air.

Back in the parking lot, the kids heard Rufus squawking and then saw him fly straight up from the roof.

"Uh oh," said Sawyer.

Just then the helicopter appeared over the building.

"There it is!" he shouted. He steered it back towards them. But something was wrong. It was coming too fast—and directly at their heads. "Look out!"

Sawyer and Hazel dove toward the pavement. Yanking the controls had no effect. The helicopter was wobbling like crazy. It plunged to the ground and landed with a loud CRASH.

Hazel looked at the smoking wreckage and couldn't help but smile. "That was awesome," she cheered.

Before Sawyer could say anything, a car pulled into the parking lot leading Sawyer and Hazel to scramble to their feet. It was Phoebe.

Hazel waved as Phoebe parked and stepped out of her car. "Phoebe, I flew a helicopter! It flew right over the building and disappeared and—"

"Your dad called," Phoebe said rushing past her. "Something's up with Winter."

Sawyer had picked up his helicopter but switched his attention to Phoebe. He shared a look with Hazel and they hurried after her inside.

CHAPTER 8

That. That right there." Clay pointed to the X-ray pinned to the light board. "That's the bulge we saw yesterday."

Hazel looked up to her father. "What is it? Is it bad?"

"It's scoliosis," Clay explained. "It's a kind of damage to the ligaments and the muscles around the spine."

Sawyer furrowed his brow. *How could Winter have damaged her spine?* "From the crab trap?" he asked.

"From swimming," Phoebe told him.

But Sawyer didn't understand.

"A dolphin's spine is meant to flex up and down, not side to side," Clay went on.

"But that's the only way Winter *can* swim," Hazel interrupted.

"I know, but she's not built to swim that way. And it's damaging her back," said Clay.

Sawyer thought hard. "But . . . what's the worst that could happen? She'll have a bulge. That's not so bad."

Clay and Phoebe shared a look. They knew this wasn't going to be easy.

Clay took a deep breath. "Her spinal cord is just like ours. It controls everything—her movements, her heartbeat, even her breathing. If it gets damaged—"

Sawyer looked from Clay to Phoebe. "You're saying—swimming is going to kill her?!"

Clay couldn't bear the look on the kids' faces. "We can give her exercises. Try to correct it . . . but . . ." He stopped. He realized it didn't matter what he said. They all knew Winter was in trouble.

*   *   *

"If he doesn't want to see us, why are we even here?"
Sawyer sat in the front seat of the car talking to his
mother. He felt lousy ever since he heard the news
about Winter. And now his mother was dragging
him to see his cousin—who didn't even want to
see him! Lorraine parked the car in front of the VA
hospital. It looked like a small college campus. Patients
sat reading on benches and strolling across the lawn.
A large group of vets were playing basketball on a
court nearby.

Lorraine looked at her son. "It's not that he doesn't
want to see us . . ."

Sawyer shot her a look. Kyle hadn't returned any
of his messages. But Sawyer was definitely getting the
message.

Lorraine sighed. "Your aunt and uncle thought
seeing you might cheer him up."

A few minutes later, Lorraine and her son entered
the main lobby of the hospital's residential wing.
The building was buzzing with activity. Veterans

sat watching TV, playing on their computers, and chatting together in small groups. Two young men directed Lorraine and Sawyer to Dr. McCarthy's office where Kyle had an appointment.

Over in the doctor's office, a grouchy old man in rumpled clothes—Dr. McCarthy—was kneeling in front of Kyle muttering to himself. Kyle sat in a wheelchair silently while Dr. McCarthy fiddled with the plastic prosthetic on his left leg.

"If they'd just make the stupid parts the way I tell 'em to . . ." said the doctor grunting. He took the brace off and banged it on the floor trying to get it to bend into position. "For Pete's sake, I'm not tryin' to send a man to the moon here."

Neither the doctor nor Kyle realized that Sawyer and his mom were in the doorway. Sawyer stood in silent shock. He had never seen a doctor's office like this before. It looked more like a mad scientist's workshop. Sawyer took in the shelves of artificial arms, legs, hands, and feet. He glanced over at the plastic leg brace in the doctor's hands. Then he moved his gaze to his cousin's leg.

At that moment, Kyle looked up and noticed his cousin and aunt standing in the doorway. His face hardened and his muscles tensed. Without even saying hello, he slapped his hands on to the wheels of his chair and rolled back.

"Oh!" Lorraine gasped. "Sorry . . . uh . . . hi, Kyle. . . ."

Kyle stared at the ground, fuming.

Dr. McCarthy looked from his angry patient to the woman and young boy standing in the doorway. "Well, don't just stand there. Come on in," he said waving them in. "I'm Dr. McCarthy. And you are . . . ?"

Lorraine nudged her son a bit further into the office. "I'm Kyle's Aunt Lorraine—and this is his cousin, Sawyer."

Kyle sat motionless without saying a word.

"Ahh, 'family.' Very healing. Or so I'm told. . . ."

Dr. McCarthy stood up and walked over taking Sawyer's hand. "God does quality work. Don't know if I can beat that," he said examining it. Sawyer and Lorraine were at a loss.

"Let's see here." Dr. McCarthy walked over to his shelf of body parts. "Left foot, right foot—" he glanced at Sawyer. "Stop me if you see anything you like. Oh, here's a beauty," he said picking out a plastic hand. He held it in front of Sawyer. "High five."

No one was amused.

"You shouldn't be here," Kyle muttered.

Lorraine feared she had made a huge mistake bringing Sawyer. She felt terrible. "We just wanted to make sure you're—"

Kyle cut her off. "—Well I'm not. Okay?"

Lorraine and Sawyer flinched.

"Just leave me alone."

Dr. McCarthy cleared his throat. "Ah, sorry. Shrink's up the hall. I only do bodies—not heads. I'll let you all work this out without me. We'll finish up later, Kyle." He grabbed a greasy bag off his desk and headed to the door. "The chili burger," he said lifting the bag. "Best American invention since jazz," and then he was off.

The family went quiet. "Look," Kyle began raising his eyes. "I don't know why you came. But now that you've seen me—" He paused. "Or what's left of me, please go."

Sawyer couldn't take it anymore. "Fine!" he yelled. "Whatever." He turned and stormed off toward the door. But when he got to the hall, he turned back around to face his cousin. "Did you ever think that this might be hard on *other* people? Besides *you*? Did you?!" Without waiting for an answer, he took off down the hall.

Lorraine caught up to her son in the hospital parking lot. Sawyer hardly noticed. His mind was racing as he stomped towards the car. He knew Kyle hadn't wanted to see his family, but he couldn't help but hope that when Kyle actually saw him, he'd be happy. Didn't Kyle realize how much everyone had missed him and had worried about him? He didn't even get to tell his cousin about Winter. Kyle barely even *looked* at him.

"Sawyer—" Kyle had wheeled out to the parking lot and was squinting in the bright sunlight.

Lorraine looked at her son. She saw his face soften. "Go," she told him. "I'll wait in the car."

Kyle wheeled himself to a bench next to a green lawn. Sawyer went and sat beside him.

"Look," Kyle began. "It's not you, okay? This is just . . . hard. I need some time."

Sawyer looked down at his cousin's leg. "But you're gonna be okay, though. Right?"

"They're going to try another operation. Try to give me back some feeling," Kyle answered.

"But you're gonna walk again?"

Kyle shrugged. "They . . . think so."

Sawyer looked puzzled. "But what about swimming?"

Kyle put his hands back on the wheels. "Tell my mom and dad I'm doing okay, will ya?"

Sawyer watched his cousin wheel himself back inside. But then the vets playing basketball beside the lawn caught his eye. It was a fast-paced game. A patient wearing a big grey sweatshirt faked a pass to a teammate standing to his left. When a patient on the opposing team ran to block the pass, he threw the ball to another player standing open by the hoop. The teammate caught the ball, spun around, jumped up, and dunked the ball through the hoop. *SWOOSH!* Only when his teammates were giving the guy a high-five did Sawyer realize that the patient who scored the basket had a prosthetic arm.

Impressed, Sawyer stood up to meet his mother at the car. He wanted her to watch how well the patients could play with their prosthetic limbs before she drove him back to the Marine Hospital to help Winter with her physical therapy. But sitting at the bench across from him was Dr. McCarthy. He was reading a newspaper and using a prosthetic arm as a paperweight. And then suddenly, an idea flashed through Sawyer's mind.

Sawyer took a deep breath and went over to Dr. McCarthy. "Excuse me, sir? Can I ask you a weird question?"

An hour later, Dr. McCarthy and Sawyer walked across the roof deck of the Marine Hospital.

"I'm looking, and I'm listening. That's it," the doctor told Sawyer.

"I understand."

"No promises," Dr. McCarthy reiterated.

Just then Clay came out of his office. He stopped when he saw the boy with a stranger.

"Um . . . Dr. Clay? This is Dr. McCarthy," Sawyer said introducing the men.

Clay shook the doctor's hand. "Hello. What can I do for you, Doctor?"

Dr. McCarthy stole a look at Sawyer, puzzled. "I thought I was here to do something for *you*."

Both men turned to look at Sawyer. He looked at Clay but his words caught in his throat. He glanced at Dr. McCarthy who hadn't laughed in his face when he talked to him about Winter. So Sawyer mustered up the courage to explain his idea. He looked back to Clay and began, "I was afraid you'd say no. . . ."

Clay didn't say no. Before long, Dr. McCarthy was rolling up his pant legs and stepping into the pool. Clay and Phoebe positioned Winter on a platform so the doctor could examine her while Sawyer chattered on without taking a breath. "—and you should see what these guys with prosthetic arms and legs can do. They run, they jump. It's incredible."

Dr. McCarthy crouched down by the dolphin. He looked up at the specialists. "Does she bite?"

Phoebe smiled and shook her head.

The doctor began studying Winter and feeling around her body. After a moment, he stood. "Well . . . first of all, she's as slippery as a greased pig," he said to the small crowd. Then more to himself he said, "And where the heck do you put it? There's nothing there. What do you attach it to? How do you keep it on?"

Sawyer was crushed. Dr. McCarthy stepped out of the pool still muttering.

"It's preposterous. It'll never work. Putting a tail on a fish . . ." He shook his head. "Nobody in their right mind would even attempt it." The doctor paused to take off his glasses and rub his eyes. "Luckily, I'm not."

"Not . . . what?" asked Sawyer anxiously.

"In my right mind," the doctor replied with a grin.

Sawyer pressed on. "You're saying . . . you'll try?"

Dr. McCarthy turned to Clay. "Well, I have a vacation coming up. But no promises."

Sawyer was thrilled. He wanted to give Dr. McCarthy a hug but he saw Winter swimming up.

"Dr. McCarthy—!" Sawyer shouted.

SPLAT!

It was too late. Winter had squirted a mouth full

of water and drenched the doctor all over. The team froze. Horrified.

"Uh . . . that means she likes you," Sawyer said with a hopeful smile.

Dr. McCarthy wiped his face and shook the water from his hands. "Imagine my delight."

CHAPTER 9

A few days later, the team assembled in Clay's office to examine Winter's X-rays and ultrasounds. Clay and Phoebe had gathered skeletal models, diagrams, and text books for Dr. McCarthy to study.

"Hm . . ." Dr. McCarthy said rubbing his hand through his hair. "They're not so different from us. There's a similar bone structure."

"But their skin is hypersensitive. She might not tolerate anything against it at all," Phoebe noted.

"Well, then that's our first step," Dr. McCarthy decided.

Just then, Sawyer and Hazel came in and handed the doctor a chili burger.

"I should probably tell you—" Clay addressed Dr. McCarthy. "We're pretty strapped for cash right now."

"No problem. The less I make, the less I pay my ex-wife," he joked. The doctor took a big bite out of his burger. "Right, then. I'll need a cast of Winter. From the cast, we make a mold. From the mold, we make a socket to attach the tail. And most importantly, keep those chili burgers coming."

The days that followed passed by in a blur. Sawyer and Hazel helped soothe Winter while the doctors coated her stump with a gray sticky substance to make a mold. Phoebe showed Dr. McCarthy hours of computer-animated video to help him understand a dolphin's spine when swimming. They studied the video frame by frame to figure out each small movement of a dolphin's tail when it moved forwards, backwards, left, and right.

Next they thought about tail designs. *What shape would best simulate a dolphin's tail? How will it attach to Winter's body?* They sketched various models — some with single rod shafts, others with hollow ones. They built prototypes with hinges and belts. Everyone had an idea of what would work best. The team brainstormed, argued, and discussed every detail.

Finally they had something they all agreed on. They would fit a molded cap onto Winter's stump. Twin shafts that would best replicate a dolphin's flukes would be attached to the cap. Lastly, they would cover the shafts with plastic flukes.

There was just one problem.

They needed someone to make everything.

Dr. McCarthy sat at his desk in the lab a few days later. Across from him, Ron Montoya, a man in his forties sat wearing a suit.

"So, what is this you need?" Ron asked.

Dr. McCarthy got straight to the point. "I need you to custom-make some parts for me. It's like nothing we've ever made before . . . and it may not work . . . and I can't pay you."

Ron laughed. "Other than that, it sounds great!" he joked. Dr. McCarthy laughed along with him, but Ron knew he was serious about the task. "Okay, who's the patient?"

Dr. McCarthy held up a photo. It was a picture of Winter wearing a big goofy grin.

It was late when Dr. McCarthy left his lab that night. On his way out he noticed the light on in Kyle's room. He looked in to see his patient sitting in front of his computer. A news article was open on his screen showing a picture of Donovan Peck holding a big trophy next to the headline, "New State Record in 400 meters."

"Bad news?" asked the doctor.

Kyle turned to the doorway and closed the page. He shrugged. "Doesn't matter."

"How's the leg holding up?"

"It's fine."

Dr. McCarthy walked across the room and grabbed a soccer ball. He let it fall to the ground and kicked it over to Kyle. The patient looked down at the ball on the ground.

What was the doctor thinking? Kyle thought, annoyed. "What am I supposed to do with that?"

"Kick it," the doctor answered. "As hard as you can."

Kyle glanced at all the fragile objects around the room.

Dr. McCarthy interrupted Kyle's thoughts. "Don't worry about breaking anything. I have insurance. Stuff breaks."

Kyle gave the doctor a suspicious look. "I don't think that's how insurance works."

"Probably not. But kick the ball anyway."

Kyle hesitated but started to stand. He wobbled on his leg brace. Giving up, he sat back down. *I can*

barely stand. I can't even kick a stupid ball, he thought. "I can't."

"I see . . . Tell me then. What hurts more? Your leg—or your pride?"

Kyle looked away. This doctor didn't know anything about him. "My whole life, all I wanted was to do one thing," he said quietly.

Dr. McCarthy was unsympathetic. "And now you're going to have to want something else. Lucky for you, you've got about a million to choose from. . . . Listen," the doctor's voice softened. "Just because you're hurt, doesn't mean you're broken."

"Trust me. I'm broken."

The room was quiet for a second. Then—

SMASH!

Kyle looked up startled. Dr. McCarthy had taken an empty glass from his desk and thrown it across the room where it shattered.

"No. That's broken," the doctor said lightly. "Go home to your family."

Dr. McCarthy was up early the next morning. He arrived at the Marine Hospital loaded up with various steel cases, and armfuls of tools and other gear.

After he had laid out all of his equipment on a table in front of Clay and Phoebe, he grabbed a steel case. Inside was a gel sleeve.

"We use the same stuff we use for humans," the doctor explained. "It'll protect Winter's skin. And then we attach the prosthetic right to it."

A few minutes later, Phoebe worked the liner onto Winter's stump. The dolphin grunted. *Was she going to reject it?* Everyone held their breath as Phoebe slid Winter into the pool. When Winter wiggled through the water as usual, they let out a collective sigh of relief.

Next Dr. McCarthy opened up another case revealing a makeshift prosthetic tail. He had assembled parts from various human prosthetics to form a tail-like piece. "I whipped this up from parts off an old car. It's stiff but it's something. Anyway, we can try it while the real parts are being made."

The team took the tail to the pool. Sawyer stroked Winter's head soothingly while the others strapped the tail to the sleeve on her stump.

"All right," Phoebe directed. "Let's get her into the water."

Carefully, Clay and Sawyer slid Winter down the platform until just her tail was in the water. Winter craned around trying to see what was on her stump.

"Come on, fish," Dr. McCarthy said under his breath.

"It's okay, Winter. Come on," Phoebe whispered. She used hand signals to gesture for Winter to move her tail up and down. "Tail up, tail down. Just like we practiced."

Winter looked at Phoebe, then wiggled her tail from side to side.

"No, Winter. Up and down. Up and down."

But Winter was starting to get annoyed. She twisted again, trying to see what was on her stump.

Suddenly, she thrashed and wrenched herself out of Clay and Sawyer's grasp.

"Winter, no!" Phoebe shouted.

The dolphin squealed and propelled herself further into the pool. She shook violently from side to side trying to get the tail to come off. Panama, who had been swimming on the other side of the pool, squealed in fear. Winter rushed to the edge of the pool and smacked her tail against the wall over and over again.

"Get it off her!" yelled Clay.

Phoebe swam over as fast as she could but Winter was thrashing too violently. Phoebe couldn't reach the tail. The group was helpless as the dolphin smashed the handmade prosthetic, breaking off the straps. As the broken tail sank to the pool floor, so did the spirits of everyone watching.

CHAPTER 10

So many things were weighing on Clay's mind as he worked at his desk later that day. Sawyer and Dr. McCarthy had raised his hopes for Winter's survival, but after today, he was even more concerned. It didn't help that he had to keep dodging the president of the board of directors' phone calls. Clay turned on the TV and put his head in his hands. *There has to be another way to save the hospital*, he thought.

"—reporting live from the Gulf Coast, this is

Sandra Sinclair," a voice from the TV announced. Clay looked up.

"Tropical Storm Leroy, now churning across the Gulf of Mexico with winds of up to 80 miles an hour, has just been upgraded to a Category 1 hurricane—"

Clay leapt out of his chair and ran to tell Phoebe.

When Clay got outside, he could already see dark gray clouds rolling in overhead. The hospital workers got right to work, carrying in the chairs and tables, latching the shutters on the office windows, and taking down all the signs and displays that could fly off into the animal pools. Meanwhile, Reed made sure the houseboat was securely tied to the dock.

Sawyer was helping tie down the awnings when Clay told him to go home.

"What about the animals?" Sawyer asked.

"They'll be fine. We're gonna stay with them."

Sawyer nodded and headed home. Lorraine rushed him inside as black clouds covered the house. Across the street, a car was pulling into the drive-way. Kyle was coming home. Max and Alice hurried over to help him out of the car. They handed him his crutches and he limped into the house while the winds whipped through the trees.

The storm crashed through the town, smashing palm trees and flooding the streets. Every building took a beating from the harsh winds and stinging sheets of rain. The giant "Clearwater Marine Hospital: Rescue, Rehab, Release" sign on the roof of the hospital building was thrown into the air and landed in the parking lot with a loud clang.

On the roof, Winter and Panama bobbed their heads over the water's surface. They took deep breaths, then dove deep where the water was calm. Inside the hospital, Clay, Phoebe, and Hazel watched the animals through the windows. Rufus stood beside them and squawked while outside the winds howled.

The next day, the sun shined brightly. The air was calm. Tree branches and random debris were strewn about the parking lot along with the wrecked hospital sign. Clay surveyed the damaged pumps and filters behind the building. He took in the sight of the white rescue truck crushed beneath a huge fallen tree and let his head fall into his hand. *Now what were they going to do?*

Up on the roof, Phoebe and the others were checking on all the animals. Winter and Panama swam to the edge of the pool squeaking. Phoebe stroked the tops of their heads. "Good girls," she said and fished out a palm frond that had fallen in the water.

Everyone worked to clean up the effects of the hurricane and soothe the animals. Phoebe and Hazel stayed with Winter while Clay and Reed put the tables back in place. Sawyer was busy collecting piles of fallen palm fronds and stuffing them into a trash can when he saw another set of hands holding leaves come into view. He looked up. It was Kyle!

"Figured you could use a hand," his cousin said. Then he shrugged, adding, "And maybe one good leg." After a second, Kyle broke into a smile. Sawyer threw his arms around his cousin and hugged him tightly.

When he finally let go, Sawyer turned to the others. "Clay, Hazel, Reed! This is my cousin, Kyle."

"Welcome." Clay came over and shook Kyle's hand. "We've heard so much about you."

"It's an honor to meet you, son," said Reed.

"Sawyer said you were a real jerk at the hospital," Hazel stated.

"Hazel—!" Clay cut off his daughter.

But Kyle just laughed. "Yeah, well. He was right." Then he glanced around the roof deck. "So, where's this famous dolphin I keep hearing about?"

Winter was drifting along in the water as the gang approached. Kyle had improved greatly and was walking with his leg brace just slightly unsteady. The dolphin swam over to the edge of the pool, curious. Kyle looked at her a moment, then struggled to kneel. Sawyer reached over to help, but his cousin just waved him off. "I'm okay," he said.

Winter wiggled in the water and made some clicking sounds.

"Hold out your hand," Phoebe suggested.

Kyle had never touched a dolphin before. He slowly reached out his hand towards the animal. Winter put her rostrum right against his palm, nuzzling it. Mesmerized, Kyle stroked the dolphin's head and she whistled with contentment.

In the meantime, Gloria Forrest was leading another board meeting—this time without Clay.

"First guess is what?" she asked.

"Including structural damage, the truck, the rescue equipment, and the electrical systems—the costs will be something in the range of five hundred thousand dollars," said John Fitch.

One of the other board members spoke up. "We're checking with FEMA now. But they're not hopeful they can help us. And our insurance is barely enough to cover minimal repairs . . ."

"So," Gloria continued. "This storm was—"

"—the straw that broke the hospital's back." John concluded.

The room was silent.

"So we're all in agreement then?" he prodded. "We go ahead with the sale? All in favor, raise their hands."

One by one, the members of the board raised their hands.

John nodded. "I'll call Philip Hordern and tell him."

Gloria sighed. "I guess that leaves me to tell Clay."

"Mr. Hordern's offer is still on the table," Gloria said to Clay as they stood by the rooftop pools.

"I told you to reject it," Clay replied as if the subject were closed.

"We did . . . and he came back and offered more." She paused. "Clay . . . We've found homes for every animal here. And, as we've said, Mr. Hordern is willing to pay to move—"

Clay interrupted her. "Including Winter?"

Gloria stood silent.

"Then we haven't found homes for every animal, Gloria."

The board president was frustrated. She knew it wasn't an ideal scenario but it was the best they could possibly hope for. *Didn't Clay realize how hard everyone was working to find a reasonable solution to their financial troubles?* she thought. "No one wants to take on a dolphin with her issues," she tried to explain. "And frankly—maybe we shouldn't have taken her on either."

Gloria regretted what she said as soon as she saw Clay's look.

"Clay . . . I promised you I'd tell you when our backs were against the wall. Well . . . they are."

Clay took a deep breath. He knew that this wasn't what anyone really wanted. But he couldn't help trying one last time. "Dr. McCarthy is looking into new materials. He thinks he might have a new tail ready by—"

But Gloria just shook her head. "—And if Winter rejects that one too? And the one after that?"

"She won't!" Clay persisted. "If you just give me a little more time, I swear—"

"I'm sorry, Clay. But I can't. It's over. We need to think about putting Winter down. It's . . . the kindest thing we can do."

o!!!" Hazel cried. "But you CAN'T!"

Clay put a hand on his daughter's shoulder. "Hazel, I don't have a choice. . . ."

"Of course you do," Sawyer insisted. "Dr. McCarthy says we only need—"

Clay knew this was going to be impossible. He looked at Sawyer. "We're out of time," he said. "And money. We have to close down." Sawyer's mouth was agape. He couldn't believe what Clay was saying. "I'm sorry, kids."

"But, Dad," Hazel looked toward the pool where Winter was swimming towards them. "What about Winter—?"

Clay rubbed his forehead. He paused and looked deep into his daughter's eyes. "I don't keep secrets from you, Hazel. I never have." His tone was serious but when he saw his daughter's lost expression, he softened. "I'm telling you this . . . so that you can start to say your good-byes."

The sun was just starting to set when Sawyer headed home at the end of the day. He walked his bike through the hospital parking lot. The day's news weighed on him heavily. He couldn't understand anything—not the hospital closing, not waiting to try the new tail on Winter, and most of all, the idea of giving up on Winter entirely. He pulled to the side when a mini-van drove up into the parking lot. A well-dressed woman parked the car and stepped out.

"Excuse me," she said approaching Sawyer. "Is this the Clearwater Marine Hospital?"

Sawyer nodded. "Our sign blew down . . ."

"Oh!" The woman sighed with relief. "Thank you! We drove all the way down from Atlanta in one fell swoop, and I swear, if y'all were closed, I would've just curled up in a little ball and cried!" she said breathlessly.

Sawyer stood wide-eyed.

When the woman caught her breath, she added, "We've come to see the dolphin."

"Her name is Winter, Mommy."

Sawyer looked to see there was a pretty six-year-old girl in the back seat of the minivan.

"Her cousin was here with a school group and told us about her. Ever since then, it's all my daughter talks about. Then after the storm, we went online to see if she was okay, but we couldn't find anything," the girl's mother explained.

"She's fine," Sawyer volunteered. "All the animals are."

"You think it'd be all right if Margaret and I just had a little peek?"

The boy figured they *had* driven all the way from Georgia. "I guess so," he said.

The woman smiled and opened the van door. It was then that Sawyer realized that Margaret was in a wheelchair. Her mom operated the van's lift and lowered the girl to the level of the parking lot. Not only did Margaret use a wheelchair, but she also had one prosthetic leg.

Sawyer's jaw dropped but he recovered quickly when Margaret looked at him and smiled shyly. "Hi . . . I'm Margaret," she said.

"I'm Sawyer," he said quietly. "Uh . . . Let's go inside. I'll show you around."

In a few minutes, Sawyer was leading Margaret and her mom through the hallways of the hospital. He took them to the windows that viewed under the water of Winter and Panama's pool.

"I don't see her," Margaret whispered.

"Just wait," Sawyer said with a smile.

Then—there she was. Winter came swimming by

and glanced at the window. Seeing Sawyer with the others, she started wiggling over.

Margaret gasped. "It's Winter!" She put her hand on the glass and Winter bumped the window with her rostrum.

"Mama . . ." Margaret said, fascinated. "She's just like me."

Winter spun around and swam a few feet back. Then she wriggled back flapping her pectoral fins. Sawyer looked at Winter wiggling her stump through the water. Then he moved his gaze to Margaret's prosthetic leg.

An idea was coming together. Within seconds, Sawyer had it all figured out.

* * *

Margaret's mother pulled out of the parking lot and Margaret waved happily at Sawyer. He waved back, then ran to the marina. He had to talk to Clay immediately.

Clay, Hazel, Phoebe, and Reed were on the back deck of the houseboat staring at Sawyer. The words came tumbling out of his mouth. "—but you said there wasn't a solution. *This* is the solution!"

"Sawyer, there are financial realities you don't under—"

"—Yes, I DO understand. I understand that we need money. I get it. But *Winter* can raise a lot of money!"

Clay didn't know what to say. He thought the kid was nuts. He looked to the others for help, but no one spoke up.

"That lady drove eight hours just to bring her daughter here—" Sawyer went on.

Hazel was getting excited. "—and other people would do that too, if they knew about her—"

"Which is why we need a website—" Sawyer said explaining further.

Hazel started talking faster and faster. "—with a webcam. People can log on and watch her. Twenty-four hours a day if they want. Sawyer knows how—"

"—and people can make donations—"

"—and we could have a fund-raiser! With games

and food! And everybody could see her new tail!" Hazel exclaimed.

Clay held up his hands. "Look, kids. I'm really proud of you. Those are great ideas. But they're just not realistic."

Reed watched his son reject the possibilities.

"It wasn't realistic to save Winter in the first place," Sawyer countered. "But you did it."

"I'm sorry. I really am," Clay shook his head. "But it just wouldn't be enough."

Reed watched his son reading on the back deck of their houseboat hours later. Above him, stars filled the night sky.

"Remember that poem I used to read when you were little?" Reed asked, coming out to sit by Clay.

Clay put down the accounting book he was reading.

The men shared a slight smile with each other then looked up at the stars.

"You're a good sailor, Clay," Reed went on. "You

know the sea and sky better than any man I ever met. But . . ." He turned to his son. "You are sorely lost now, son. You're giving up. Because you're afraid you can't save her. And you don't want to watch that happen again."

Clay lowered his eyes.

"Well . . . Winter might die," Reed said. "I don't know . . . But I do know that you can't give up on her. Not yet."

Clay nodded his head slowly.

"You never gave up on Hazel's mom. It was the bravest and most beautiful thing I ever saw." Clay's shoulders stiffened at the memory.

"Just 'cause we haven't arrived where the star is pointing us—doesn't make it the wrong star. That dolphin's taking us *all* somewhere. We just haven't figured out where yet."

The two men looked back up at the stars and watched the bright lights shine.

In the garage, Sawyer sat at his workbench. He laid his head on his arm and fiddled with one of his toy helicopters indifferently. He thought working on one of his gadgets might distract him, but he couldn't take his mind off the hospital. *How could they even think about closing down the hospital?* When he started thinking about Winter his eyes started filling with tears.

"Okay . . ." Clay said interrupting Sawyer's train of thought. Sawyer looked up and saw Clay leaning against the doorway. "So talk me through this fund-raising stuff again."

Over the next week, Sawyer and Hazel took the lead in organizing the hospital fundraiser. They converted the conference room into a planning headquarters. Hazel wrote to-do lists on whiteboards and delegated tasks to all the staff and volunteers. They had to sell tickets, make signs, stock food booths, and set up a raffle. Sawyer helped make sure that Winter would be ready for the big day. He called Dr. McCarthy for constant updates on the dolphin's new tail. Phoebe worked with Winter on exercises to train her stump to move up and down. And Clay's job was to urge the board of directors to give them more time.

"A little to the left—" Hazel said looking at her laptop screen one afternoon. Behind her, Sawyer stood on a ladder adjusting the camera he had strapped to the roof.

"Try zooming in!" Sawyer shouted.

Hazel clicked a button and the camera zoomed in on Winter swimming in the pool.

"Slide it out a little more . . . a little more . . . no, more!" she yelled staring at the screen.

Sawyer leaned out to move the camera farther . . . then a little farther . . . and a little farther. "Aaaaah!" he cried as he fell past the camera and right into the pool beside Winter. *SPLASH!*

"Uh . . . nevermind!" Hazel called out a little bit too late. "Oops," she muttered.

While everyone was working at the hospital, Kyle was on his own mission to help sell tickets. He entered the newsroom just as Sandra Sinclair, the local newscaster, was finishing up. She looked up from her news desk and noticed Kyle standing by the cameraman—on crutches. She caught a quick look down to his legs and noticed his brace.

Kyle cleared his throat. "Uh . . . I'm here to cash in that rain check," he said.

Sandra looked up at him and smiled.

Later that evening, Hazel and Sawyer were still hard at work. They sat at Sawyer's computer printing out flyers on brightly colored paper. Some featured a photo of Winter under the big headline "Come to Save Winter Day!"; others displayed a photo of the team with Winter and Panama in the big pool.

Kyle opened the door to the garage and called over to them. "Hey, you guys. Come in quick. You might want to see this," he said with a big smile.

Sawyer and Hazel shot each other a look. *What could it possibly be?* They hurried into the house and saw Max, Alyce, and Lorraine already gathered inside. Kyle went over to the TV on the counter and turned on the news.

". . . just months ago, little Winter was found tangled in the ropes of a crab trap, her tail seriously damaged," Sandra Sinclair announced.

Sawyer's jaw dropped and he turned to look at his cousin. Kyle ruffled his hair and gestured for Sawyer to keep watching.

"Rushed to Clearwater Marine Hospital, it appeared she might not survive . . ."

Sawyer couldn't believe the footage that was being shown—on the news! He watched a video clip of the day Winter was rescued on the beach and even saw himself standing in the background.

". . . but the plucky animal did—although her tail didn't. And without a tail how could she swim?"

Video of the dolphin swimming without her tail filled the screen as Sandra continued telling Winter's story.

"Well, she taught herself to—with a wiggling motion moving her stump side-to-side."

In Clay's office, the staff of the hospital crowded around the television.

". . . and with the help of the staff at Clearwater, Winter has thrived. But it's not a happy ending yet. That unusual swimming motion is damaging her spine. And it could lead to paralysis."

Over at the VA hospital common room, Kyle's friends looked up at the TV screen.

"The solution? A prosthetic tail to help her swim normally. Much like an artificial limb would be used by a human patient. And with the help of prosthetic designer Dr. Cameron McCarthy—"

At hearing their doctor's name, the patients cheered.

Down the hall, Dr. McCarthy sat in his lab watching the news. He had the brand new prosthetic tail and a chili burger beside him.

"—they're trying to do just that. But it'll take time—and money. So Winter's best friend, eleven-year-old Sawyer Nelson, has come up with a great idea. A website, seewinter.com, with a live webcam—"

A webcam? The doctor was intrigued. He turned to his computer and typed in the web address and saw Winter floating in her pool!

"—so you can log on and meet this remarkable animal for yourself."

"Ha!" the doctor smiled. "Well, all right . . ."

"Or better yet, come meet her in person—with her brand new, state-of-the-art tail—on 'Save Winter Day,' Saturday the 27th. And as an added bonus—"

Back in the Nelson kitchen, the others still had their eyes glued to the TV.

"—you'll be treated to a very special sporting event. Two of our nation's top young swimmers, Kyle Connellan and Donovan Peck, have agreed to race head to head—"

Sawyer was stunned. He turned to his cousin. "Really?!" he exclaimed.

"—or tail to tail, if you prefer. It will be a special

grudge match with all the proceeds going to benefit Winter and the marine hospital. So come meet two of Florida's best young athletes, and one heroic little dolphin. I guarantee she'll steal your heart—just like she did mine," Sandra concluded.

Sawyer ran over to Kyle and wrapped his arms around him tightly. *Everything is going to work out,* Sawyer thought. *It is all coming together.*

Things were really ramping up. The workers and volunteers worked harder than ever to get ready for the big day. Hazel and Sawyer watched the bleachers being set up then ran over to the pool where Dr. McCarthy had just arrived.

"All right everyone," Dr. McCarthy said putting down his steel case. "Cross your fingers and toes if you got any." He put the case down and opened it. The titanium shafts for the prosthetic tail gleamed in the sunlight. The white plastic flukes were delicately shaped but looked strong. "The flukes are smaller now. There's more bend in the joints. It should feel a lot more natural," he explained.

"Let's bring her up," Clay told Phoebe.

Phoebe signaled Winter to come up to the pool's platform. Clay, Dr. McCarthy, and Sawyer joined her. Together they strapped the new prosthetic tail to the gel liner on Winter's stump. They tightened the buckles while Phoebe and Sawyer stroked her head and body keeping her calm.

"It's on," Clay said. "Let her go."

The team helped slide Winter into the water. Then Phoebe gave her the hand signals. "Up and down, Winter. Up and down," she instructed.

Winter looked at Phoebe and squealed. She swam towards her by wiggling her new tail side to side.

"It's okay, Winter. Just try," Phoebe continued.

But Winter just let out a piercing squeal. She lurched away from Phoebe wildly waving her prosthetic tail from side to side and headed for the pool wall.

"Winter, no!" Sawyer shouted.

But it was too late. Winter squirmed to the edge and smacked the tail against the concrete wall.

BANG! BANG!
SQUEEEEAL!

Hazel covered her eyes. Winter kept smashing the tail against the wall until the buckles broke and the tail flew off her. The parts that had been so shiny in the case just minutes before were now bent or broken. Just like the first one, the tail sunk to the pool floor.

That evening, Sawyer sat by himself at the pool's edge. Most people had gone for the day, discouraged by the failure of the new tail. Sawyer slowly kicked his feet in the water while Winter and Panama drifted through the pool.

"No, I don't feel like it," Sawyer responded when Winter came swimming up to him with a yellow duck ring toy around her rostrum. Winter watched him for a moment then slipped off the toy. She whistled.

"Winter, no. Stop it," Sawyer said with a scowl.

But instead Winter took a mouthful of water and raised herself up almost eye-level with Sawyer.

"Cut it out, Winter! Didn't you hear me? I don't want to play."

The dolphin looked at the boy and spit the water back into the pool, still watching him.

"You don't know what's going on, do you? I thought dolphins were supposed to be smart," Sawyer muttered. "Why can't you understand? This weekend is really important!"

The animal sighed and came closer. She nuzzled Sawyer's leg trying to get him to pet her.

"No! Stop it!" Sawyer barked leaning towards her. He gestured to the gel liner she still wore on her stump. "If you don't wear your tail, you'll die! Don't you get it?!?" The lump in Sawyer's heart was too big. He wiped the tears spilling out of his eyes. "Why won't you just wear it?" he pleaded.

The dolphin drifted off to the other side of the pool and circled back to Sawyer. When she reached him, she spun around placing her stump against Sawyer's leg.

"Cut it out," Sawyer said.

But Winter just grunted and kept rubbing against Sawyer's leg.

"Ow, stop, Winter!" The gel liner rubbing on his leg was making him more irritated. "Why do you keep—?"

Sawyer glanced at his legs and stared at the animal. She grunted. "You're telling me, aren't you?" Sawyer said. "You're telling me!" He jumped to his feet to go find Dr. Clay.

"Dr. Clay! Dr. Clay!" Sawyer ran down the marina towards the houseboat. Clay was surprised to see Sawyer this late in the evening.

"Sawyer, what is it? What's wrong?" he asked.

"It's not . . . the tail," he panted. "It's . . . the sock. It's like . . . a seatbelt!"

Clay was totally lost. "A *what*?"

Sawyer caught his breath. "When it rubs. It's like a seatbelt. It's not the *tail* we need to fix. It's the *sock*!"

CHAPTER 12

*B*efore they knew it, the day had arrived. A "Welcome to Save Winter Day" banner flew high in the sky. The parking lot was jam-packed with cars and school buses. Huge groups of children and families lined up excited to enter the hospital.

Inside, people milled about enjoying all the different tanks and displays. They shopped in the gift store which were filled with Save Winter coffee cups, hats, and stuffed animals. The old fisherman who had first found Winter wandered through the crowds marveling at all of the photographs and merchandise. When he saw a volunteer collecting donations for Winter's new tail, he dropped in a fifty dollar bill.

"Thanks!" said the volunteer. "That's very generous."

The fisherman smiled. "Let's just say that Winter and I are old friends."

On the rooftop, crowds surrounded the pools. Next to the big pool was a sign saying, "Feed a Fish to Panama." Kids waited eagerly for their turn to pick up a fish and hold it over the water. Panama happily did her part—bobbing up to gulp down each fish.

The area behind the hospital had been transformed into a fairground. Hazel worked a food booth selling her "world-famous lemonade icicles." Next to her Alyce and Max scooped chili on "Dr. McC's Chili Burgers." In another booth, kids giggled as they played "Pin the Tail on the Dolphin."

And near the marina, Kyle and Donovan warmed up in preparation for their big race. Clay and Reed had moved their houseboat to be parallel to the race course. Volunteers had set up the marina by placing two starting blocks on a floating dock.

Lorraine was stepping through the bleachers when she saw Mr. Doyle, Sawyer's summer school teacher, trying to make his way through the seats while holding a hot dog.

"No, stop. *Shoo!*" he muttered to the pelican trying to snatch his snack.

"Oh, Mr. Doyle!" Lorraine said in surprise.

The teacher looked up quickly but Rufus grabbed his pant leg in his beak and tugged.

". . . I . . . I read Sawyer's essay," he struggled to say while trying to fend off the pelican. "It's—it's quite good. And, I heard about today and thought I'd come out and . . . Get away!" he shouted kicking his leg in the air. "And—I think, given everything he's done here, we can probably get him credit for summer school."

"Really?!?" Lorraine exclaimed. "That's so wonderful. In that case, I'll call off the bird. Shoo, Rufus! Go away, now," she said to the pelican.

The bird studied her for a moment, then flapped his wings and flew off. Lorraine was secretly surprised that the pelican seemed to have listened, but she saw that Mr. Doyle was impressed. She smiled confidently. "I'll call the school on Monday to make sure we're all set. Enjoy the show, Mr. Doyle."

Back over by the food booths, the members of the board stumbled through the groups of families waiting in all the different lines. Gloria was astounded by the turnout. While John Fitch finished up a call on his cell phone, Gloria overheard a group of kids chattering about Winter. They all held the flyers with Winter's photos on them.

"I watched her on my computer and she really can swim!" explained one little girl to another.

"That was the lawyer," John said hanging up the phone and breaking through Gloria's thoughts. "The deal's done. It all belongs to Philip J. Hordern now."

Gloria nodded looking around and taking it all in.

"Gloria . . . A bake sale isn't going to fix this. We did the right thing."

"Did we?" Gloria asked and shook her head. "I'm not so sure."

Meanwhile, Clay, Phoebe, Hazel, and Sawyer had roped off the pool in the medical wing. "She's nervous about the crowd," Phoebe said stroking Winter's head from the edge of the pool. Suddenly, the sound of the crowd got louder.

"'Scuse me, coming through. Coming through!" Dr. McCarthy shoved his way through the mass of people carrying his steel case. "What a mob," he said when he reached the pool.

"Is it done?" Sawyer asked anxiously.

"Can't a man collect his breath for a minute, before you start bombardin' him with questions?" He grunted. "It's in there," he said pointing to his case.

The team gathered and opened it. Inside were the repaired titanium and plastic tail and a brand-new white gel liner.

"I must've tried twenty different formulas, but I think maybe we got something. It's a silicone elastomer. Salt-waterproof, extra sticky, and softer than a lamb's bottom.

Hazel reached out to touch it and nodded.

"I call it 'Winter's gel,'" the doctor went on. "And I'll tell you: If the fish doesn't like it, I'm puttin' the tail on and swimmin' with it myself!" he said with a huff.

The crew positioned Winter on the pool platform and slid on the new gel liner. Then they strapped the tail to it.

"How's she doing?" Hazel asked.

Sawyer stroked Winter's head. "Okay so far," he replied.

"Give her a minute," Clay instructed when the last strap was fastened.

The dolphin craned her neck to see her new tail. Phoebe and the others moved back and let her slide off the platform into the water. Once her body was completely submerged, she turned to look back at her new tail once again. Hesitantly, she shook it.

"It's okay, Winter," Phoebe said.

Winter shook it again—harder this time.

"Just try it," Sawyer said softly. "Swim a little."

"Up and down," Phoebe gestured with her hands. "Just like we practiced. Up and down."

Winter floated in place and looked at her friends. Their eyes were all focused on the prosthetic at her back. She moved it up a couple of inches, then back down again.

Sawyer kept his voice calm. "Atta girl."

"How does that feel?" Phoebe probed.

Winter seemed undecided. She moved the tail up and down a little bit more. Phoebe went to stroke her back but Winter thrashed abruptly. She jerked away from Phoebe and Sawyer, squealing.

"Nooo!" Phoebe commanded.

But the dolphin wouldn't stop squirming and squealing. From above the pool, Hazel covered her mouth. *Has it failed again?*

Suddenly, Winter stopped. She convulsed her body and her tail made one big up and down movement propelling her forward.

"There it is. She did it," Clay declared.

Winter did it again. It almost looked like an involuntary twitch.

"Yes, Winter," Phoebe was encouraging. "Up and down. Up and down."

"That's it, Winter! That's it!" Sawyer said, his voice getting louder and louder. Winter was now moving through the water with ease.

"She's got it," Clay cheered.

Dr. McCarthy pumped his fist in the air. "Swim, ya dumb fish! Swim!"

And Winter did.

But Winter wasn't the only swimmer. Over at the marina, Kyle and Donovan were just about ready for the race. Kyle adjusted the plastic brace on his leg.

"Now listen," Kyle told Donovan. "Don't you dare go easy on me."

Donovan smiled but before he could even reply, Sandra Sinclair came up to them. "Good luck today," she said. "Both of you."

Kyle brightened when he saw her. "Well, I hope

you enjoy the show." He looked Sandra deep in the eyes. "And thanks for everything."

Sandra shrugged it off. "I'm the reporter who got the exclusive. I should be thanking you. See you out there." She smiled and walked back to her post with the camera man.

Finally, it was time for the big showdown. Clay, Sawyer, and Hazel stood on the floating dock ready to announce the two competitors.

"Everything ready?" Clay asked the kids.

They glanced around at the bleachers full of people and the news crew lined up on the marina with cameras aimed at them. They both nodded, too nervous to speak.

Clay beamed. "Listen, I just wanted to say how proud I am of you kids. You never quit on Winter, and you never let yourselves quit. Today belongs to her—but also to you. Whatever happens, you'll always have this day. Now—" he grabbed the microphone. "Let's see some swimming."

"Thank you, everyone." He turned on the microphone and addressed the crowd. "Thanks for coming. My name's Clay Haskett. Welcome to the Clearwater Marine Hospital. I want to start by introducing our swimmers, Donovan Peck and Kyle Connellan."

Donovan came out and stepped on to the dock followed by Kyle. On seeing Kyle, the crowd burst into applause. And then, one by one, the audience started to stand. Sawyer looked out and scanned the crowd. He saw the swim team standing on the bleachers; his mother stood next to Max and Alyce; and there in the front, little Margaret stood cheering on her one prosthetic leg.

"Before the race begins," Clay went on. "I'd like to take a moment to thank one more person. Someone, without whom, we wouldn't be here today—my good friend, Sawyer Nelson."

Huh? Sawyer thought when he heard his name. He was sure Clay was going to talk about Dr. McCarthy. But Clay handed him the microphone and encouraged him to say something.

"Uh . . ." Sawyer started. "I don't know what to say . . ." He cast a quick look at his mother who nodded. "But I do know that it's not me that made this day happen. We're here because of the most amazing animal, and friend, I've ever known. I hope you love her . . . as much as I do. 'Cause she and I are family now. And . . ." Sawyer looked at his cousin. "And family—is forever."

The crowd erupted into wild applause. Donovan and Kyle took their places on the blocks as Coach Vansky explained the race.

"400 meters out, around the buoy, and back. Got it?"

The young men nodded.

Vanksy lifted the starter's pistol.

BANG!

Donovan and Kyle dove in. The race was on! The senior student pulled ahead immediately, but his opponent wasn't far behind. Kyle's strokes were natural and he moved smoothly through the water kicking his leg brace behind him methodically. The crowd was on their feet cheering for the two swimmers. Soon, they were neck and neck. Then, Kyle started to veer off course puzzling the audience. *What's happening? Where's he going? Is he ok? He seems to be heading towards the houseboat. But why?*

All eyes were on Kyle when he pulled himself out of the water and onto the deck of the houseboat. Except Donovan's. He was just getting to the buoy and about to turn back around when he realized Kyle wasn't anywhere near him. He stopped and looked around and saw Kyle waving to him from the houseboat. *What was he doing? What was going on?!*

"Oh, did I forget to mention that this was a relay race?" Kyle shouted with a playful grin.

Donovan was completely lost. Before he could figure out what was happening, he heard Sawyer whistle. He turned back to the shore and saw Sawyer standing next to Phoebe and some of the other hospital workers on the shore. In the water besides them was an empty stretcher. Suddenly a huge force leapt out of the water. It was Winter! She breached high over the surface of the lagoon with her new tail waving strongly behind her. She landed back in the water with a huge splash—and started swimming right towards Donovan. *She* was going to finish the race!

Donovan dunked his head back into the water and started swimming frantically toward the floating dock. In the distance, he could hear the crowd roaring. A second later, Winter zoomed past him pumping her tail up and down. She was out of Donovan's range within moments. Stunned, Donovan stopped swimming and just treaded water. He lifted up his arms in mock defeat and laughed knowing he could never out-swim a dolphin!

Just then Winter came swimming back around and splashed him with a mouthful of water.

BRAAAAP! Her raspberry sound made the audience roar with applause and laughter.

With the excitement of the attention of the spectators, Winter was eager to show off even more.

She burst out of the water and breached right over Donovan's head.

"Ladies and gentlemen," Sawyer declared. "Winter—and her new tail!"

The crowd went wild.

A few minutes later, Donovan swam over to the houseboat.

"Didn't think you could beat me without some help, eh?" Donovan joked from the water.

Kyle shrugged. "Figured you'd feel better getting beaten by a girl," he teased back holding his hand out to help pull Donovan up out of the water. Donovan took it and yanked Kyle right into the water with him. They both came up sputtering and laughing.

Back over on the floating dock, Sawyer and Hazel watched the two swimmers kidding around in the water. The kids looked at each other happily. They had pulled everything off. Hazel held up her hand for a high five. Sawyer hit her hand so hard that she almost fell into the water. He reached out to catch her, pulling her close to him. But before he could feel embarrassed, Hazel just grinned and gave him a shove—and they both fell laughing into the water! Soon enough, Dr. McCarthy was cannon-balling into the water followed by tons of kids who had been watching from the shore.

Lorraine observed her son splashing in the water surrounded by all the kids. She chuckled when she saw Dr. McCarthy fighting a splash war with a group of ten-year-olds. She walked over to Clay who was standing aside. "Clay . . . I just wanted to thank you. This summer has been incredible. Before Sawyer met you all, he was . . . in his own world. . . ."

"Good thing, too," Clay replied. When he saw Lorraine's look of confusion, he went on. "No one in 'our' world would've thought to put a prosthetic tail on a dolphin."

The two parents looked back at the children in the water and smiled.

Over in the water area, Sawyer was looking for Winter. He swam away from the packs of kids, and scanned for his friend. But he couldn't see her anywhere. Just then, Winter exploded from out of the water. She was breaching higher than Sawyer had ever seen. The crowd gasped as they watched her sailing over the water waving her new tail proudly behind her. When she landed, her huge splash drenched everyone in the crowd.

"I'd say she's a hit." Gloria said approaching Clay.

He turned to her smiling, but realized Philip Hordern, the developer was standing behind her.

"Dr. Haskett?" the developer began. "I'm Philip Hordern. Just wanted to tell you how excited I am to buy the place."

Clay recoiled. He immediately looked to Gloria who just lowered her head.

"It's . . . official?" he asked them in disbelief.

"Yes, sir," Philip confirmed.

Clay nodded slowly. He started to reply when three young kids came running up to the developer.

"Grandpa! The pelican was chasing us!" a little boy exclaimed.

"Yes, I saw that, kiddo," he said putting a hand on the boy's shoulder. He turned back to Clay and Gloria. "The trouble is . . . I have this terrible planning department. Just awful."

Clay was confused. *So the man buys the place and doesn't even have a plan for what to do with it! What kind of deal did the board make with this man?* He thought.

"Might take 'em twenty years to design the hotel. Maybe more . . . So I guess you may as well stay put. Seems to me like y'all are doing a pretty good job."

Was he saying . . . that they could keep the hospital open after all? Clay was stunned. "Uh . . . thank you, Mr. Hordern. Thank you."

"In the meantime," Philip continued, "here's a little something to help you keep up the property." He put a check in Clay's hand.

Clay lowered his eyes and looked at the amount. His jaw dropped. When he looked up Philip Hordern was already walking off with his grandkids, and

Sawyer was standing in front of him. He had heard everything. Sawyer looked at Clay and his face broke out into a huge smile.

"WOOHOOOOOOOO!" Sawyer shouted running back towards the water. He dove back in.

SPLASH!

Sawyer hit the water and swam right down to the bottom where Winter was floating with her brand new tail. The dolphin used her rostrum to bump Sawyer's hand. Sawyer reached out and pet her gently under the water. Winter twirled around gesturing for Sawyer to follow her. She blew a huge ring of bubbles encircling them like a giant hoop. The bubbles disappeared as the two friends swam through the ring. Together they swam for the surface. Even though they were from different worlds, they had saved each other and became family. And family is forever.

Dolphin Tale

Inspired by a True Story

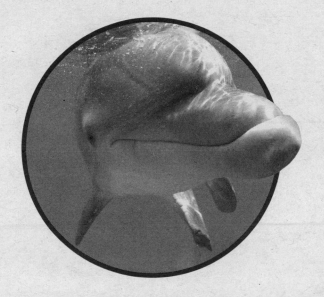

The real Winter is happy, healthy, and lives at the
Clearwater Marine Aquarium in Clearwater, Florida. You
can visit her there or view her online at SeeWinter.com.

The special silicone gel sleeve developed for Winter
is now making prosthetic limbs more comfortable for
human — and animal — amputees.